# Ethereal Wood

First edition published December 2019

This second edition published January 2020

*Special thanks to my beautiful family: Ally, Hannah, Aaron, and Jessamine—and to Frank Dewhirst, Pauline Lake, Rosemary Dupays, Andy Humphrey, and Kylie Anderson for your continued encouragement and support.*

*Dedicated to my eldest daughter Hannah—this one is for you, sweetheart.*

# Contents

# 1

# Leaving London

A grey day reflecting grey people. Rain ran down the street in small shining rivers which burst their shimmering banks to form rainbow pools where the water mixed with oil and trembled with the hiss of each passing car.

The glitter of Christmas in the shops did not radiate warmth today. People hurried, their faces set grimly; queues were forming for passengers to drip onto already late buses. The Underground was temporary escape, providing hot blasts of tunnel air. On the tube train, some sat engrossed in newspapers or magazines, while others behaved nervously, catching the eye of another and then looking quickly away, searching for a space which would not intrude; re-reading adverts and the map of Underground stations.

Marcus was pleased to be leaving the city after spending the start of the Christmas holiday with his grandparents. It wasn't that he didn't enjoy their company; more that he disliked the squeeze of London and the crowds of pulsating inner-city people who steamed in the cramped heat, and threatened to engulf him.

As the tube train progressed under protest in the murmuring tunnels, it became less crowded, and Marcus felt more at ease. His thoughts returned to the night before the visit to his grandparents, and to the shooting star which he had seen from his bedroom window as it had arched through the winter sky and crashed, sparkling, into the silhouetted trees of the nearby woods.

Marcus had crept out of the house—like an intruder in reverse—to avoid waking his parents, carefully leaving the front door on the latch, following the road to the last street-lamp which threw soft light to the edge of the field.

The still air had hung in a haze of incandescent sulphur which seemed to lead to the centre of the wood. Normally Marcus would not have dared to venture into the wood alone at night. All manner of creatures were thought to inhabit this childhood playground, where many adventures had been imagined and invented during seemingly endless summer holidays spent with his close friends.

In the drip of the black trees, Marcus had put visions of tortured faces and the sticks of clutching hands scratching at him in the gloom to the back of his mind. In curiosity, he pushed forward, intrigued by the strange scent which hung in the air, fine drizzle clinging to his hair and eyelashes. As his sight grew more accustomed to the dark, it seemed that the bruised air was suspended in the night which mixed with the scorched atmosphere and became stronger as Marcus progressed.

Close to where Marcus judged the centre of the wood to be was a clearing which contained a group of hollow tree trunks, referred to commonly in his circle of friends as the Pogles Logs. As children, they had been convinced that this was where the popular children's television series characters had lived.

When he had reached the edge of the clearing, he stopped abruptly—and, almost tripping, found support with the slender trunk of a sapling which shook and showered him with drops of rain. It ran slowly down the back of his neck, causing him to gasp and shiver with discomfort.

Not more than three metres from where he stood lay a bright, smoking object which glowed as if it were molten red hot. As Marcus stared—half in fear, half in wonder—the glow of the object threw soft, eerie shadows against the logs by which it lay, and Marcus could visualise nightmare faces staring back at him: hollow eyes, and the mouths of monsters champing and searching for a morsel of boy with which to satisfy their perverse appetites. Now his heart was thumping and rising, and he feared his breathing might sound loud enough to give away his whereabouts to whoever, or whatever, wished to seek him out.

After a minute or so—which to Marcus felt more like half an hour—curiosity gained the upper hand, and he cautiously approached the glow, treading carefully until it was only an arm's length from him. From here, Marcus could see that the object was like a strange, radiating stone, which looked as dangerously hot as lava—but when he reached out slowly to touch it, it was as cold and smooth as glacial ice. Placing this strange prize in his pocket, Marcus had turned, plotted his exit from the wood, and sped away as fast as he dared to the relative safety of the fields, the reassuring glow of the street lamps, and back to his house in Kingsley Road. It was while he was on his way home that a second glow tore through the sky, arching its way through the dark blue-black midnight glint, streaking towards the centre of the wood.

As Marcus felt for the stone in his pocket, the tube train arrived at Victoria, and with the sigh of one disturbed from far-away thought, he reached for his travel bag and searched for his ticket, which was in the same pocket as the stone. The two were extracted together—and it was then that Marcus noticed with dismay that the stone had lost its unearthly glow, and was now a dull, Brighton beach grey, and certainly not a prize worthy of being shown to the others.

## 2

# The Lightning Tree

The three friends sat on the Lightning Tree in the middle of the field. The great oak had crashed to the ground at the height of a summer storm a few years ago, and now served as a useful meeting point; a place to talk, to ponder, and to use as a home-base for the group when they played Forty-Forty, a slightly more grown-up version of hide-and-seek, normally reserved for darker winter evenings when the field—and especially the wood—provided excellent cover for those hiding.

"I think I'll go back before it gets too dark." June shook the chestnut fringe from her eyes, and paused to see whether John and Ed would accompany her. For the past ten minutes, they had been making plans for a fishing trip to Bury Hill, and showed no sign of wanting to head for home just yet.

John looked up. "We'll stay a bit longer—do you want to meet back here? Is seven o'clock OK for you, Ed?"

Ed nodded. "That'll be fine. I'll call round for you at about ten to."

"OK, I'll meet you back over here with George." June leapt from the lower end of the Lightning Tree, and headed off towards the edge of the field, her breath steaming as she went; the chill in the air making her eyes and nose sting and her face glow. It was only four o'clock by the time she reached home, yet darkness had closed in already, and she was pleased to reach the warmth and security of indoors.

As evening tumbled down, John climbed down from the Lightning Tree and started to build a small campfire. Ed dropped to help, and within a few minutes, they were warming themselves by the reassuring flicker of flames and the crackle of wood.

"When is Marcus due back?" Ed wondered. "It must be quite soon."

John nodded. "The day after tomorrow, I think, and if George can't make it for Forty-Forty, it'll be hardly worth playing."

"You're right," Ed agreed. "It's a shame the others don't come out so much."

By "others", Ed was referring to friends peripheral to the nucleus of the group; sometimes by their inclusion, numbers could swell to double figures, but that tended to occur mainly in the summer holidays when they would congregate by the river swing, launching themselves for hours on end from the banks of the

River Mole, clinging precariously to a rope suspended from an overhanging oak tree. George had daringly attached the rope to a sturdy branch some six metres above the river, and it was almost a monument to his tree climbing skills.

There were two manoeuvres which could gain a swinger maximum credibility—the first of which was to take a run-up, then swing from the bank, and jump to the other side, which was, effectively, an unexplored no man's land. This involved considerable skill in judging take-off speed and timing the release of the rope to enable the swinger to jump safely to the opposite bank. The second manoeuvre was known as a *round-the-world*—in which the swinger would run along the riverbank, away from the tree, and swing out in an ellipse across the water and round to the other side of the trunk. A more daring version of this move was to swing directly back to the tree and push off with the feet. The risk involved here was the necessity to approach the tree feet-first as opposed to slamming dangerously into the base back-first; and, of course, whichever manoeuvre was chosen or invented, a tumble into the river meant instant ridicule.

As Ed reflected, he recalled with a smile the dunking Dave had suffered last summer, when his inexperience on the rope had left him stranded and dangling directly above the river, so that the only option had been to lower himself into the murky water and wade for the bank, emerging muddy and dripping as he scrambled to safety amid jeers and laughter from his mocking spectators.

John and Ed shared the joke while the fire dimmed and the embers glowed like dangerous jewels. Then, from the corner of his eye, John sensed a different source of light, and turning so that he faced the wood, he could see what appeared to be an aircraft searchlight scanning the ground. Only there was no sound of a plane or helicopter, and the beam did not seem to project from a particular point. It was just *there.* Ed, realising John's surprise, turned also—and as he did, the light cut a sweeping arc across the field parallel to where the two sat.

"What is it?" Ed whispered. He felt an irrational fear; after all, it was only a search light, but he too had observed that it had no apparent source, no operator—and yet it continued to make urgent, controlled sweeps of the field, and as it swept closer, the light was as intense as a thousand flash-bulbs exploding inside their heads. John tried to spread the ashes of the fire with his feet, and dived for the cover of the hollow section of the Lightning Tree's lower trunk. Ed followed, and they lay speechless and confused while the beam continued its search. And then, in-between each sweep of the brightness, an unearthly whining thud could be heard, moving from near to far at incredible speed, its vibration echoing through their hearts like a heavy bass tremble.

From the light of the scattered dying embers, Ed could see John's eyes, wide and frightened. They dared not even whisper to each other. For a terrifying moment, John feared that they had been located. The beam cut across the Lightning Tree and then focused on the remains of the fire. The brightness intensified, and the occupants of the hollow tree fastened their eyes so that they would not be reflected. The quick-moving thud became a metallic icy clang which whined through their heads and jarred their teeth like a manic dental drill. Just as it seemed that the light and sound would engulf them, the beam moved on. The unbearable noise lingered momentarily and then faded. As John and Ed looked out from their shelter, the beam hovered above the wood and then sank beneath the trees. All was quiet.

"What was that?" John breathed, not expecting Ed to have a clue.

"Search me," came the response. "What shall we do now?"

"I reckon we should run for it; I don't fancy hanging around here in case it comes back." John shook his head in an attempt to rid himself of the still-painful ringing in his ears.

Without a word, the two rolled from the hollow, then raced fleet-foot—as had Marcus three nights before—to the field's edge and towards home.

At the centre of the wood, an arc of light shimmered and breathed upwards, then sank, sparkling like angel dust to the ground.

They ran flat out all the way to where John lived, just around the corner from George, June, and Marcus, who all lived next door to each other. Their feet slapped the pavement, echoing around the street and sounding like hot pursuit, which spurred them on even more. Only at John's drive did they pause, breathless and momentarily unable to discuss what they had seen. Fright was slowly replaced with excitement.

"It could have been a UFO," Ed said as he wheeled his push-bike from the alleyway. "I mean, there's no way that was a normal search light."

John agreed. "And what about the sound? It makes my teeth grate just thinking about it."

"We should tell the others, although I wonder if they'll believe us." Ed paused, leaning against his bike. "Do you think it's safe to go over tonight?"

John hesitated. "I'm not sure. Let's call round for George and June instead of meeting by the tree."

"OK. I've got to move or I'll be late." Ed was in the saddle now and checking his lights. "I'll be back at about ten to seven."

The two parted company, heads whirling with a thousand thoughts; John trembling slightly as he walked around the side of the house towards the back door; Ed skimming his way through the quiet Horley streets, turning a corner at the Rainbow Pub into Charlesfield Road and cutting through the recreation ground and on to where he lived in Sangers Drive. The air pinched at his face, feet, and hands—and his bike tyres hissed as they cut through sections of sparkling frost.

# 3

# Forty-Forty

Pausing at George's front door, June gave a tug on a string which hung from his bedroom window. This jangled a set of keys at the opposite end and George's smiling face soon appeared at the window above.

"Hi, June!" George threw her the front door key. "Come on up."

"Thanks." June turned the key to open the door, and was immediately flattened by Shadow, who barked excitedly and lavished her with canine affection.

"Get down!" she squealed without really meaning it, and then turned to climb the stairs to George's room where she handed him back the key. The unique door-entry system had been devised to appease George's mum who, until its introduction, answered the door to a multitude of callers, nearly all of whom were friends of George—who either couldn't hear, or pretended not to hear, the sound of the door knocker above the volume of his record player.

Tonight the stereo was indeed loud; so, foregoing any conversation, June sank into a chair and looked around, smiling as she did, for the room was about to be decorated, and the walls, having been stripped of wallpaper, were embellished temporarily with autographs, strange poems, and other gems of wit added by visitors.

George was a few years younger than the others, though his appearance and manner would not have given this away. He framed a word as if about to shout, then, thinking better of it, turned down the volume on the stereo.

"So where are John and Ed?" he asked.

"They said to meet by the tree at seven o'clock," she replied.

George grinned. "So Forty-Forty tonight, is it? It won't be so good without Marcus."

There was another jangle on the keys, and when George looked down again from the window, he could see John and Ed stamping in the cold iron light below.

"Hurry up, George, we're freezing out here!" John deftly caught the door key, and he and Ed were quickly upstairs with Shadow bounding after them.

"I thought we were meeting you there," said George as he began a mock wrestling match with Shadow.

"That's right, but something happened that we

think you should know about." Ed explained, and he and John went on to relate the earlier events of the evening.

George and June listened without interrupting while the appearance of the beam was described in earnest; the sincerity of the account soon dispelling any suspicion of fabrication. When John and Ed had concluded, George was first to speak.

"Are you sure it wasn't some older kids trying to scare you, perhaps with a powerful torch and a few of them running around making scary noises?"

Ed and John looked at each other. "No way, George. If you'd been there, you wouldn't think that," Ed replied.

"How about aircraft lights?" June suggested. "You know how close we are to Gatwick."

"We thought of that too, but ruled it out; as we said, the light didn't appear to have a source and the noise that came later was everywhere and nowhere and moving all around..." John's voice evaporated as his fear returned.

"How about playing Forty-Forty but not going right into the woods? You said the light settled in the middle," George said, keen to become involved in the mystery.

June was less keen. "I don't fancy going anywhere near the place."

"Don't worry—we'll stay in teams of two," George

reassured her. "What do you say?"

"Alright, but I vote you two hide first," John replied, turning to Ed for support.

"Suits me." Ed nodded.

They wrapped themselves against the cold before leaving George's house, and within a few minutes, arrived at the edge of the field. The moon was almost full, giving the night an eerie silhouette daylight feel, and there was a mist rolling like a ghost in the direction of the river. Nobody spoke while they crunched through the iced diamond grass. The Lightning Tree was reached without incident.

"When you're ready, we'll start counting." Ed was keen to get the game underway just to keep warm.

"OK, we're off. Stick together, June." George moved away from the Lightning Tree which was now Home Base. The idea of the game was to return to base without being tagged by the Hunters; anyone tagged was required to join the hunt, and with two hunting two, the odds were not in June and George's favour.

After a count of fifty, Ed and John were ready to pursue, and immediately adopted a tried and tested tactic of one covering base and the other searching. In this game, Ed covered while John crept away from the Lightning Tree like a frozen grouse-beater.

George had adopted his favourite tactic of *roosting*. On the edge of the wood, he was perched halfway up a tree with June a couple of branches below. They were undetectable—and if it wasn't for the cold, they would have waited patiently, hoping the hunter guarding the base would be tempted away, enabling them to make a break from cover. They sat silently, George with a near perfect view of the field, while John combed the more obvious hiding places.

"What's happening?" June whispered. She had reservations about being even this far from the centre of the wood, although her apprehension was slowly fading in the absence of the mysterious light described by John and Ed.

"John's coming towards us—Ed's still covering base. We'll have to sit tight a bit longer." George would have ventured further into the wood without hesitation. Although only thirteen, he possessed keen mental and physical agility, and was not easily scared; and he was loyal to June, for they had grown up together alongside Marcus and John. Ed had joined the group through knowing John and Marcus at school and the bonds of friendship were now firmly fixed.

John stood at the edge of the wood, pausing to adjust his eyes to the gloomy interior in contrast with the moon-lit field. He advanced no further; and Ed, becoming chilled and impatient by the Lightning Tree, moved slowly away to his right. When his circulation had returned, he doubled back and hid behind a bush, eyes scanning the trees from where he was sure June and George would make an eventual break.

When it came, he saw them much later than he had anticipated. George had judged well the distance to base compared to Ed's position.

"Forty-Forty home!" June and George slapped the Lightning Tree as Ed lunged desperately, almost tripping in his haste. John had missed the break from cover but heard the base calls and returned disappointedly from the far end of the field.

After an hour of Forty-Forty, nothing unusual had occurred. An invitation for coffee at George's was quickly accepted, and the remainder of the evening was spent playing cards, diverting thought from John and Ed's earlier encounter.

# 4

# Train of Thought

At Victoria Station, it was busy; the crowds swelled by Christmas shoppers from the suburbs who would no doubt return in a couple of weeks for the January sales. Marcus dodged his way around piles of rubbish, pecking pigeons, people, rattling collection tins, and the homeless: for whom Christmas promised no special warmth or holy shine. Before checking the time of the next train to Horley, he stopped to buy a cheeseburger which tasted like paper and plastic, although probably not quite as appetising.

Having purchased a ticket, there was not long to wait. The train left from Platform 18 and was scheduled to stop only at East Croydon and Redhill, before reaching Horley and thence to Brighton.

Marcus sat by the window, chin in hand, facing the train's direction as he always felt ill travelling backwards. He looked out as London faded and stations flashed by, filed away as the train progressed, people guessing each other's lives and luggage while they sped closer to Christmas, leaving the capital grey and dripping.

Marcus glimpsed rows of tumble-down terraced housing, graffiti walls, traffic below bridges, and increasing amounts of countryside as the train reached outer London; the rails snaking ahead, whipping and lashing in a blur as Marcus stared in a dream downwards.

By Redhill, he was in familiar territory. This was the town that was fast becoming Surrey's last stand against the spread and sprawl of outer London. To Marcus it was old but friendly, and also where his father worked at Paul Allen Farm Produce situated on the hill at the edge of town. He had fond memories of previous school holidays accompanying his father while he delivered produce to London and the South-East. It was a fixed delivery run for each day of the week, and Marcus soon became familiar with each route—his favourite being the coastal run: heading down Balcombe Road, stopping for a cheese roll in Brighton, making other deliveries along the coast, and loading the lorry with tomatoes before returning to Redhill. The various shop owners often gave Marcus snacks en route, and the music on the radio flowed as warm as the days which were filled with the aroma of potatoes, cheese, and eggs drifting from the back of the lorry. The feel and scent would stay with him always, for it was earthy and good and friendly.

Now his father was Buyer for the company, and to Marcus, it seemed he led a far less interesting working life confined to the office.

Now the train was nearing Horley, flashing through Earlswood and Salfords, and beginning to slow as Horley came into view. Carriage doors clanked shut as Marcus climbed the stairs to the exit and out into Station Road. It was drizzling as he descended into town. Car brake lights glowed in the sizzle of traffic which dripped at the traffic lights, where the smell of fresh fish floated from Bunkles; then coffee, warmth, and cream cakes from Clark's; fruit and vegetables and Christmas trees from the greengrocer in the town centre.

At the shop where he had bought his first record, Marcus crossed the street—and turning into Queens Road, he took the soggy short cut which brought him out onto Brighton Road opposite the recreation ground.

It was almost deserted in the steady drizzle, save for a woman pushing a pram through the puddles and a red setter sniffing around the big slide at the far end of the park.

This was the park that could be transformed in summer by the arrival of the fun-fair; its gaudy lights and amplified booming music, playing out-of-date hits in an atmosphere of fun, hot-dogs and candy-floss. It was also host to the Horley Carnival every

June; largely a fundraising event which began with a mid-morning procession of floats, which attracted, it seemed, thousands of people to line the Horley streets—and bring traffic and normality to a halt. This was followed by the Carnival's array of stalls and side-shows in the recreation ground: girls in summer dresses, men in the beer tent, and children riding the miniature steam train.

Marcus reached the end of Charlesfield Road. He crossed Horley Row at the Rainbow Pub, opposite the small parade of shops, and cut through the new estate towards which he still felt a certain hostility. It had been developed at the expense of a great deal of field and woodland opposite Kingsley Road, destroying the childhood recreation of an entire generation, and the natural habitat of a wide range of wildlife. He had literally grown up in the long since flattened and scraped countryside. The wood and field that remained were but a small percentage of what had existed, and they presumably had not suffered the same fate because of their proximity to the flood plain of the River Mole.

Here was where, as a child, everything had seemed huge and alive and vital; fresh, leafy, and completely absorbing and friendly. Until it was taken away. Massacred by progress; men with measuring sticks, bricks, bulldozers and scaffolding. Men with roll-up cigarettes, Tizer bottles and pay packets. The children first realised their land was under threat when the surveyors began measuring with angles, poles, and string. Uprooting the poles did not appear to slow the onslaught of construction, and soon the trees were felled and burning in great fires of broken giants. The wildlife was gone, replaced by concrete and bricks and milk bottles. As he continued, Marcus also thought of friends who had moved from the area, yet still lived in his childhood's fondest memories; Dean and Tracey, the Godfreys, Lorna and Lisa, Caroline, Karen and Derek. Then there was Lola the golden Labrador whom they used to meet on summer walks with her owner. He was the man with the magic walking stick which unfolded into a chair which was supported by a spike in the ground. Marcus recalled his mother saying the man had gone to sleep one night and not woken up as she attempted to explain why he and Lola had not been seen for a while.

He reached the unmade road at the side of Dean and Tracey's house. They had moved to Wimbledon with their father years ago, but it was still where Dean and Tracey used to live, and Marcus did not know and had no wish to know the current owners.

"Hi, Mum." Marcus entered by the back door, dumping his bag and heading for his room upstairs.

"Hello! How was London, Marcus, and how are your Gran and Granddad? And you needn't think you're leaving this by the back door—or these."

His mum handed Marcus his travel bag and kicked-off shoes. "They've got a home too," she added.

"Yes, Mum." He sighed, and again headed for his room, dropping the offending articles by the cupboard under the stairs. Flopping onto the pop-star-poster-surrounded bed, he reached for his train ticket to add to the collection of souvenirs of train journeys. Again extracting the stone at the same time, he was puzzled to see that its glow had returned.

After tea, Marcus watched television. His younger brother and sister, eyes open wide with the excitement of Christmas, were seated in front of the tree which was decked with glass baubles, tinsel, fairy-lights, and chocolate Santas. At the foot of the tree lay a light covering of pine needles amid a pile of presents, which were eagerly examined by pressing and shaking when Mum was safely out of hearing range.

The doorbell chimed, and Marcus answered it to find John buried deep inside his scarf and parka.

"Hi, John." He invited his friend inside, and John removed his outer layer of clothing and balanced it on the stub of a hook which protruded from the wall. Where there had once sprouted a neat row of double hooks now remained a broken few, the majority having been snapped off by Marcus's brother and sister who had swung from them rather than descend the stairs in the normal way.

"How was London, Marcus? Did you get to see the lights in Oxford Street?"

"Yes, they were great," he replied, "but London is such a squeeze I'm glad to be back. How is everyone?"

"They're fine," John replied—although Marcus could tell from his eyes that his friend was bursting to tell him something important, but didn't quite know how to start. He could tell when John was feeling uneasy because he avoided eye contact during conversation.

"Would you like a coffee?" Marcus offered, and disappeared downstairs without really waiting for a reply.

John picked up a guitar and began to strum a few chords; then, seeing the brightly coloured object which rested by Marcus's bedside lamp, he leaned the guitar against the wall and moved over to have a look at what at first he took to be some kind of Christmas bauble. Turning it around with his fingers, he marvelled at its smoothness, and the clarity of colour in its blood-orange glow.

Marcus returned with two mugs of steaming coffee and handed one to John.

"Thanks. Where did you get this, in London?" John still held the shiny stone in the palm of his hand.

"No," Marcus replied. "If I tell you where and how, you'll never believe me."

"Try me." John was curious to know which shop the stone had come from, as it had given him an idea for a Christmas gift. Marcus raised the mug to his mouth, his face momentarily shrouded by hot vapour, and began to describe the events of a few nights ago, pausing at intervals to sip at his coffee and allow each segment of his account to be absorbed.

"The strange thing is, now the colour has returned," he concluded, waiting for John to react.

John said nothing, and the room was quiet for a few seconds. Then, slowly and deliberately, he spoke: "Marcus, there's something strange happening over there." He nodded towards the window from where the fingers of the wood's bare trees could be seen stretching to the marble sky.

"While you were away, Ed and I had the fright of our lives, although we weren't in the wood when it happened."

Now it was Marcus's turn to listen, and he did so intently while John repeated what he and Ed had told June and George.

"What do the others think—have they seen anything?" Marcus asked.

"No, it just happened once, and once was enough." John had stopped marvelling at the stone, and replaced it abruptly. "I'm sure they believed us."

Marcus paused to think, wondering whether the two incidents could possibly be connected. He dismissed the idea; as far as he was concerned, the brightly coloured stone was the very essence of shooting star, his own souvenir of far flung space rock. Perhaps its colour change had been a trick of the light, or maybe it was a substance unknown to man which changed colour depending on its surroundings. He stared at the stone which lay on the bedside table, and its glow seemed to intensify. For a moment, he felt unable to avert his gaze as it reached behind his eyes like the sun on a hot summer's day, penetrating closed eyelids; searching, shimmering and creating swimming images that required blinking away.

"Are you alright?" John broke the silence.

Marcus blinked. "Yes, I was just thinking...is anyone else coming out tonight?"

"We're meeting at George's house—that is, except Ed. He's going to a carol service with his family, but he might make it for Forty-Forty later."

"So you're not worried about being over there after what happened?" Marcus asked.

John shrugged. If he was honest, he was almost disappointed that something hadn't happened to prove their story to George and June.

"Not really. Nothing's happened since. Shall we go round for George?"

"Sure." Marcus pocketed the stone and reached for his jacket. Outside, a thin winter mist was feebly stretching its fingers. At George's front door, Marcus gave the customary tug on the string leading up to the top window.

# 5

# Carnyx

In the middle of the wood, Carnyx rested, invisible in the darkness. His journey from Future Earth had so far been in vain, and he knew it was only a matter of time before he would be followed. The balance would be affected by his absence, and they would soon realise that he had come to seek the Balance of Power; the crystallised knowledge and wisdom of the inhabitants of Earth Past, so long held by the others towards whom he had felt increasing irritation over the centuries.

Carnyx had arrived to discover bewildered thought patterns scattered about the ground where Adam had come to rest. It was immediately obvious he had not survived the journey back through time, and Carnyx was at a loss to understand why one with human form had so foolishly taken such a risk. He had noted with annoyance the absence of the stone, but detected another thought pattern. Yes—one of human form, frightened but inquisitive. The thoughts were fairly recent, but not sufficiently so to take a definite fix. However, he had taken the stone.

Carnyx had limited success with the two others whom he had scanned as they lay trembling below him in the hollow recess; eyes shut tight but minds fully open, revealing their entire lives as Carnyx read them like a fast-forwarding video played at lightning speed. They were Ed and John, close friends of Marcus, the Temporary Keeper of the Balance of Power of Future Earth. He had later probed two more human forms as they sat in a tree on the perimeter of the wood—also close friends of Marcus. Now he waited impatiently as the mist spread like a shallow mantle in the slight hollow.

# 6

# Ethereal Wood

“Welcome back, Marcus.” George was leaning out of the window, grinning as he threw down the key.

“Hi, George.” Marcus caught the key, and he and John entered the house. In the distance was the rumble of a generator and the muffled echo of a public address system.

“Father Christmas is on his way round,” John said as they entered George’s room.

“Hello, June.” Marcus gave her a squeeze and she punched him playfully.

“Well, what did you get me for Christmas?” she teased him.

“You’ll have to wait and see.” In fact, Marcus hadn’t even started buying presents, and doubted whether the others had either. Normally, it was a mad dash to Crawley on the last shopping day before Christmas, pure panic-buying, and then struggling home on either the bus or train.

“Ed’s grounded tonight; he might make it later,”

John explained. “He’s gone to a carol service with his family.”

“Well, who fancies watching Father Christmas from here?” asked George. By now, the boom of the PA was becoming decipherable, as it was only a few streets away.

*“Merry Christmas, Merry Christmas, everybody.”*

For as long as Marcus could remember, they had always waited in eager anticipation as the Rotary Club Santa did the round of Horley’s streets. Of course, as very young children, he had been the real Santa and his sleigh was real, pulled by real reindeer; not a decorated van with strapped-on wooden steeds. His arrival then, as now, sparked the realisation that Christmas Day was very close—and even at Marcus’s age, he became more excited at the prospect of being surrounded by the warmth of family and friends; the piles of hurriedly peeled off wrapping paper; the smell of chocolate, oranges, and nuts; the steaming kitchen where Mum created the family feast; and the after-meal glow as everyone sank into chairs to watch *Top of the Pops,* usually nodding off during the Queen’s speech, while the younger ones expended energy on new toys.

They took turns leaning out of the window as the flashing float edged along the street, the generator for the lights sounding like a tractor. A small army of charity collectors spread out in the wake of Santa’s sleigh, rattling coin boxes and knocking on doors. Santa's good wishes mingled with recorded carols soaring through the air, bouncing and booming back in echoes around the neighbourhood. People peered from windows and doors; grown-ups scrambling for change for the collectors; young children squealing happily at the sight of Father Christmas and his entourage as they passed down the street. When Marcus leaned out, he could see to his left his brother and sister next door but one, waving excitedly at the Christmas procession, while below at the front door was a man with a collection box waiting for his knock to be answered. He could picture his mother now, searching for change, and probably resorting to taking a few coins from the drawer in the kitchen where the school dinner money was kept.

"OK, how about tonight's game, then?" Marcus climbed down from the window.

"Sure, ready when you are." June looked to George and John.

Everyone reached for jackets and coats which were piled on the floor of George's room.

"George, can you take Shadow for a run if you're going out?" his mum asked as they slipped into boots and shoes at the front door.

Shadow pricked up his ears and trotted from the kitchen, jumping up at George as he reached for the lead which hung from a coat hook.

“Sure, Mum.” He latched the lead onto Shadow’s collar.

“And don’t be too late, George!” his mum almost pleaded as he reached for the door.

Father Christmas could still be heard as they headed for the field, Shadow straining at the lead, tugging George along as the others followed. At the edge of the field, George released him, and he bolted into the darkness, swallowed immediately by the cavernous night.

They paused at the Lightning Tree as the moon slid out from under the clouds, momentarily pouring its pale light over them.

George whistled for Shadow, and he came crashing from the outer trees of the wood towards them, panting as George scratched his head.

“Stay,” George commanded, pointing at a section of ground by the tree. Much as he loved his dog, Shadow tended to be a bit of a give-away during Forty-Forty.

“What are the sides?” John asked.

“We can mix them round more when Ed turns up,” Marcus replied. “How about me and June hunting to start with?”

“Sounds good,” John responded. “OK, George?”

George nodded—and as the two set off to find cover, the moon drowned in the sea of clouds.

“I’ll count.” June began.

Marcus strained, listening for the point of entry should John and George make for the woods, but he couldn't be sure if they had. When June had reached the count, she stayed at the base while Marcus crept away, eyes scanning and searching for any movement.

George and John had crept along the edge of the wood and entered it further up the field where they couldn't be heard. Now they doubled back, parallel to their earlier route, but shielded by the trees and sun-starved bushes and brambles which had long since yielded their summer berries.

"They've probably reached the count by now," John whispered.

George nodded. "I think you're right, and it's too late to hide up a tree now."

They stopped, straining for any indication of pursuit. There was none. Marcus was a good two hundred metres away. June was at base with Shadow, glad of the canine company, unable to see hunter or hunted.

"Do you want to split up?" George asked.

"I might sneak back out and have a crack at base from the river." John blew on his fingers in an attempt to warm them.

"Good luck. I think I'll wait around the middle for a while." George nodded in the direction of the Pogles Logs, and the two parted company.

George headed cautiously towards the centre of the wood, cursing under his breath when a stick snapped suddenly underfoot. After edging forward a few metres more, he paused by a large tree, its trunk wider than his own frame, and listened. The night was still, and he could hear the sound of his heart pumping between his ears. And then a slight shuffling sound carried clearly on the air, followed by a scuffle, like a boot making contact with a tree root. In the gloom, poor vision could easily betray; things appeared to move when they did not move, and the imagination created figures and falseness. Instead of concentrating his eyes on a particular area, George moved his head from left to right, scanning for movement. He knew someone was in the wood, but there was no further sound. George waited against the tree, and then came a shrill cry of triumph. June must have caught John, and that would mean he would now join the hunt. It was time to make a move, for John already knew George's rough location.

At the Pogles Logs, George again paused, and now there was definite movement about him: the sound of two hunters pressing towards the clearing in slightly different directions. Then there came a different sound which puzzled him immediately, for it could be felt as well as heard, like a glowing oscillating hum. Behind him, and slightly to his left, he was able to detect the faintest glimmer of light, like a dying ember of fire fighting for oxygen. Turning slowly, he faced the largest of the black logs, lying like the huge ebony bone of some vast long extinct monster. And, yes, there it was: a slight glow coming from the ground by the log! He dropped on all fours and crawled towards it, his left hand touching a stick as he did so, and halted a few feet away. With the stick, he reached out and prodded at the glow, scrabbling about in a heap of fallen autumn leaves. The glow intensified. George, mystified, leaned forward—and at that moment, the leaves appeared to melt away. There before him, shimmering and pulsating, was an orb of sulphur and orange. Unable to look away, the orb caused him to see burning and shattering stars, and to feel sensations of pain and panic, immediately followed by a feeling of soothing and cooling. It both drained him of power and flooded him with energy, and with confusion and understanding. The universe was inside his mind, receding and then accelerating in a myriad blur of galaxies.

George yelled. "Run, for heaven's sake, run!" and broke away zig-zagging, veering wildly, bouncing off trees.

Twenty metres away, John and Marcus heard the cry and the urgency in George's voice.

"Marcus!" the orb hissed, and its sound cut through the night. The voice was inside their heads, inside their entire minds, loud and commanding.

"What is it?" June was almost tearful, clutching her hands to her ears in an attempt to blot out the sound as its intensity exploded behind her eyes. Ed, having only just arrived at the Lightning Tree, was sprawled beside his push-bike. The impact of the orb's hiss, and the strange patterns glowing in his mind, had sent him crashing in bewilderment to the ground. They could hear and feel George's terror as he broke from the trees, his breath coming in sobs as he careered towards them.

Marcus and John were powerless to move, to speak, to have clarity of thought, or to possess understanding or questioning. As they stood there, helpless statues between the trees, the night seemed to heave upwards and soar over their heads.

Carnyx hovered in front of them and inside them. An intense sphere of brightness. Mesmerising, malevolent, and translucent. In Marcus's pocket, the stone began to pulsate and to grow warmer. Without knowing how or why, he was able to place his hand in his pocket, gripping the stone tightly. Its warmth was almost reassuring, and he found his mind clearing, the orb swimming in his eyes becoming less dazzling. John stood, as if in a tunnel of terror, his hands unable to grip or to seek support as his mind raced away from him, trapped and useless.

As Marcus's head cleared, the others' thoughts became dulled and stifled as Carnyx filled their minds with a seeping paralysis; George, June, and Ed by the Lightning Tree, with Shadow unaffected, yet sensing that something was wrong, whimpering quietly. John was at Marcus's side, open-mouthed and staring absent-mindedly.

"The Stone, Marcus," again the orb hissed at him menacingly. "You will return it to me at once."

Marcus did not respond immediately; the unreality of what his mind told him was real had not yet been accepted. Instead, he stared at the orb as it continued to hover; bursts of different colours running like water droplets on glass from its centre, and occasional flashes arcing from its edge like blue veins of electricity leaping at him, crackling in whiplashes. Time seemed to have stopped. Realising the command related to the stone which he gripped, Marcus framed the start of a sentence, which Carnyx had already extracted from his pool of thought.

"I have no time for explanation—just release the stone. You will not be harmed, and you will remember nothing."

Carnyx hovered closer now, growing impatient, forceful, and anxious to gain the Balance of Power of Future Earth.

Marcus could feel his mind being probed and invaded by the command to offer his hand and surrender the Stone. Instinctively, he resisted, and Carnyx sent a stab of pain which made Marcus close his eyes and shudder as it trembled from his head to his spine like an earthquake of the mind. In a slow-motion movement, he watched his hand rise from his pocket—and like a puppet without strings, his arm extended towards Carnyx, involuntarily, shaking slightly, the glowing treasure cupped in the palm of his hand.

Carnyx, satisfied, froze Marcus's position and prepared to collect his prize.

"I can't let go!" Marcus wailed in pain. "It's stuck to my hand."

Carnyx hissed in anger. "Release it or you will suffer!"

Another stab of pain seared through Marcus's consciousness. He tried to drop the object, to shake it loose, anything to be rid of the torture and conflict, and to escape the orb, which was right in front of him now, and sending painful commands which he was unable to obey.

In frustration, Carnyx realised Marcus could not release the stone; the Temporary Keeper had somehow inadvertently established a bond. Now to set about breaking it.

All at once, Carnyx became relaxed and smoothed, and smiles and happy thoughts filled all their minds, like a warm, comforting waterfall. Gentle and soothing, with lilting music and sweet fragrance. The others, released from their paralysis, were calmed, and did not question what they were not sure had happened.

By the Lightning Tree, the three friends snapped into life, as if suddenly awoken. Ed sat up, puzzled, and shook his head, before reaching for his push-bike and propping it against a tree.

They found themselves encouraged, cajoled, and propelled towards the wood. There was no conversation, but bright and happy minds as they pushed onward, slowly, silently, until they were at Marcus's and John's side. There was no fear at the orb dancing before their eyes. No questioning, no understanding.

"You will each make contact with the object in Marcus's hand," Carnyx commanded. John turned to Marcus, and reached out for the stone. As he touched it, the air crackled and the darkness receded. Carnyx found it difficult to conceal further frustration. This human had already been introduced to the Stone. If the others had also, it would be impossible to dilute its bond with Marcus. Carnyx was also aware that the laws of time could not be flaunted, and that these small, inexperienced humans could not be harmed because of their place in time and the implications for Future Earth. With Carnyx's train of thought diverted momentarily, for a split second, the children's minds returned to their own control—and George, who had first encountered the orb, felt a flash of terror which the others could again sense. Carnyx switched effortlessly back to the situation, and June reached out to touch the stone. This time, the only reaction was a slight dimming of its fluorescence, and Marcus could detect a corresponding lowering of its temperature.

Carnyx, satisfied that the Balance was about to tip, moved Ed forward. The movement of his feet and his hand stretching to the stone were agonisingly slow. Again, time shuddered, blackness slammed against an invisible wall, trembling, then rebounding and echoing. The night was torn in two. Stars were twisted and ripped like drowning sapphires. Across the severed heavens, a rush of stinging cold stream air accelerated, and a trail, like fragments of jewels, streaked towards the centre of the wood.

Carnyx concentrated, pushing against the wall of time, using his mind like a prism to refract light and power, trying to force Ed into contact with the Stone. It was useless, and Carnyx relaxed his concentration to conserve energy as Thador came flashing towards him, bursting through time and Future Earth, descending gently through the trees to rest, level with Carnyx; the two orbs together, like ghostly twins, immediately locked in mental combat, yet effectively cancelling each other out.

This time, the children were released fully from their puppeteer, and stood, amazed and confused.

"Do not be alarmed," Thador reassured them.

"What on Earth is going on?" Marcus raised his voice angrily.

"I sense you all have many questions. You will know the answers when the time is right. For now you need only to know that we are Thador and Carnyx of Future Earth, and I have come to regain the Balance of Power which is held by the one of you known as Marcus," spoke Thador calmly.

"The Balance is mine," Carnyx cut in. "You have no right."

"You have neither the right nor a claim!" Thador responded quickly, and the two visitors grew darker, their shapes swirling as they again became locked in mental combat.

"The Balance of Power!" Marcus stared in disbelief at the stone. "What do you mean?"

"Marcus, let's get out of here," George hissed, preparing to make his second hasty exit from the wood that evening. "Come on, make a break for it."

"You will stay until the Balance is decided." The harsh tones of Carnyx clanged in their ears.

"Why? We haven't done anything wrong." June strode forward, tears and anger bursting from her. Although frightened, she stopped just centimetres short of the orbs.

"June, for heaven's sake, back off!" John warned.

Ed moved to her side. "We want to go home," he protested.

"If this is what you came for, then why don't you take it?" Marcus held the stone aloft like a miniature ruby beacon. "And how did it get here anyway?"

"So many questions, young humans. To know too much may be more dangerous than to know too little," Thador replied.

"Must you talk in riddles? Let this be decided without delay." Carnyx seethed; and the evil which lurked so thinly veiled could be felt by everyone.

"If you don't let us go, out parents will soon come looking for us." June was fiery eyed, and tossed her hair to one side.

Marcus dropped the Stone at his feet, and it sizzled in the damp carpet of autumnal leaves. "Take it," he repeated. "We just want to leave."

"Neither of us can take the Balance of Power now," Thador began to explain. "You are now the Temporary Keeper."

"Well, I don't want to be. None of this makes sense." Marcus sighed, wondering if their predicament was a dream. Perhaps he could force himself to wake up, or dream of something else to provide a way out of the dilemma.

"It is no dream, young man." Thador intercepted his thoughts.

"Then what are you?" Marcus pleaded.

"We are like you, only stronger. We are the pure essence of human thought and reason in Earth's future. But there is still good and evil. One tends to follow the other. Fortunately, good has the upper hand."

"What good is good?" Carnyx mocked. "The world needs leadership and fulfilment, not your archaic, clumsy democracy."

"You mean there are no people in the future?" Ed said, horrified.

"We are people, I assure you. We have adopted a more...suitable form," Thador replied. "And now we must decide what is to be done."

The orbs darkened and sank to the ground. June and Ed turned to the others. "I can't believe this is happening to us," June exclaimed.

John agreed. "It seems useless trying to run; they read our minds at will."

"Marcus." June faced him. "It felt back then as if I could read your thoughts—just for a moment, when you were wondering about this whole situation being a dream."

"Me too," John added. "I could sense something. Not always words; more like a feeling or meaning but not expressed like a sentence."

"Thought patterns, young man," Thador boomed at them, interrupting. "It has been decided to allow you to return home while we discuss the matter further. There is to be no mention of what you have seen and heard to anyone not present at this moment in time. You are all to return in exactly twenty-two hours."

Thador paused. "Please do as I say, for if you do not, then I cannot guarantee your safety."

"What do you mean?" George demanded.

"Please, no more questions. I have bargained hard enough on your behalf. Perhaps more than you will ever know."

"Let's just get out of here." June turned on her heels and marched defiantly forward.

"Enough of this!" Carnyx was impatient. "There is much to be discussed."

"And Marcus," Thador approached him slowly, "do not forget this. Look after it, for it looks after you." The last words of the sentence were phrased for maximum impact. As Marcus puzzled at their importance, the Stone lifted from the ground, rising slowly until it became level with his shoulder. Without knowing exactly why, he reached out and plucked it from the air, before turning and following June from the wood. John, Ed, and George followed. At the edge, Ed glanced back into the darkness. There was no sign of the orbs.

George whistled for Shadow, who streaked from the Lightning Tree like a sleek, black arrow towards them. They walked in silence to the field's edge, and grouped at the first street light, their breath gathering in clouds. For the first time in ages, it seemed, they all felt cold. June shuddered in the silence as they looked out to the woods, searching, almost for proof of what had happened. Could it really be, or was this some bizarre shared nightmare?

At length, John broke the silence. "We have to do something, we have to get help."

"You heard our instructions." Marcus clicked his tongue, thinking, turning over in his mind what he now had to accept had really happened. "We're not allowed to tell anyone—not even our parents."

"Anyway, who would believe us if we did tell?" said George.

Ed checked his watch. "It must be getting late."

June agreed. "Yes, I'd better be off; we've been out for hours. Does anyone have the right time? My watch must have stopped."

"Mine, too. It only says 8:15, and that's about the time I arrived." Ed shook his wrist, then held the watch to his ear. "Oh, well, at least it's ticking now."

Marcus frowned. "Funny, I only make it 8:15 as well. It feels like it should be nearer to 10 o'clock. What does yours say, June?"

"8:15."

"Mine, too," John said, equally puzzled. "How do you know what time you arrived, Ed?"

"Well, I left home at about eight, and it's only about a quarter of an hour's ride. I was definitely here before 8:30 because I could see Minder on the TV in that house as I passed." Ed nodded in the direction of the last house in the street. They all turned to the uncurtained lounge window where Minder could be seen clearly on the TV.

Marcus shivered. “That’s impossible, we’ve been out for at least two hours.” He could feel his neck prickling as fear crawled up it once again.

“What’s happening to us?” June sank to the kerb with her head bowed.

“We need to decide what to do—we’ve got to talk it through tonight.” George looked around, seeking support.

John agreed. “He’s right, we need to stick together on this.”

“Come on, I vote we get help. We’re in trouble, but at least we’ve got away. Let’s tell the police or some-body.”

“It’s OK for you Ed; you live on the other side of town. The rest of us are about a stone’s throw from the wood. You’ve felt the power of those things. The second one I kind of trusted. Don’t ask me why, but it felt...I don’t know...genuine, almost friendly in a dis-tant way.” Marcus trailed off, realising that any hint of trust or allegiance towards what they had wit-nessed would seem strange. “Thador said the Stone would look after us.”

“All this over a silly stone—how did you get hold of it anyway?” June rose to her feet. For the second time that evening, John listened as Marcus repeated his story to the others.

"Why didn't you warn us?" Ed complained.

"How was I to know? As far as I was concerned, it was a fragment of shooting star. I didn't know it was connected with what you and John saw the other night. And it obviously isn't a silly stone." Marcus glanced at June. "It's important to them," he said, pointing back to the wood.

She shivered and sniffed miserably. "Let's go home."

"Back to mine, then?" George was keen to discuss their predicament in warmer surroundings. "Come on, we can at least make ourselves comfortable."

"Comfortable!" Marcus thought, wondering what else lay in wait, ready to pounce and kidnap them from normality.

# 7

# Kingsley Road

It started to drizzle as they headed back; the droplets hanging in sheets at the street lamps which stood like thin concrete sentries, heads bowed, and illuminating their path home like an airport runway. Windows twinkled with Christmas cheer as they passed along the rows of terraced and semi-detached houses. Fairy lights clung to walls and Christmas trees, wreaths of holly hung on front doors. Everywhere had a festive glisten, and a faint but noticeable aroma in the air: the smell of Christmas as it approached.

Marcus tried to condense the number of Christmas Days he had lived through into weeks, imagining what it would be like if those days could run consecutively, and he wondered how many future good times would slip away. Like holidays, no matter how long they lasted, you always seemed to be at the last day, reflecting on how good a time you had had, and then it was back to school, just like the break had never happened. He wondered if life was like that all the way through, and that at the end you were left to reflect on the good times before smiling and slipping into oblivion. Or somewhere else. Ed's push-bike clicked as he wheeled it at Marcus's side, ticking like a metronome, tyres throwing up spray from the shiny black pavement. This area had all been fields, and had suffered the same fate as the route which Marcus had taken earlier in the day on his way back from the station. It had taken much longer to develop, though, probably because of its proximity to the river, and had always seemed to attract the older children in the area, particularly those with motorbikes as they tore around on summer evenings, carving up the ground and leaving trails of two-stroke fumes hanging in the air. While daring show-offs performed teenage stunts, groups of girls would stand, smoking and smelling of patchouli oil, admiring their brave boyfriends, who rarely broke bones, though often bruised their bodies and their pride. And there were gangs of kids; rivals from different roads in the neighbourhood. Mock—and sometimes real—battles were sometimes staged between the young inhabitants of Meath Green Avenue, Kingsley Road and Bolters Road South.

At George's house they entered by the back door, scraping off boots against the step, eyes misting at the sudden temperature increase.

"Did Shadow have a good run?" George's mother

entered the kitchen.

"Sure, he's fine," he replied.

"Are you OK, George? You look as though you've just seen a ghost."

"Fine, Mum, I'm just a bit cold." George reached for the kettle. "We're going upstairs for a while."

"Well, keep the noise down, please," his mum pleaded as she headed back to the living room.

"Go on up." George motioned towards the stairs. "I'll bring up some coffee in a minute."

They filed upstairs to George's room. When they were all together, it was quite crowded; John and Marcus settled for the floor, Ed and June each had a chair. When George entered, he placed a tray of coffee and biscuits at his feet and sat on the bed.

"OK, George, so what happened to you?" Marcus reached for a coffee. "You gave the shout to run."

"I've never been so scared in my life." George looked around at the others as he recalled his fear. "I could see a glow in the leaves by the Pogles Logs. I knew the Forty-Forty hunt was closing in, but after John's and Ed's story, I was curious to investigate the light. I realise now that I may have disturbed the first orb. I prodded it with a stick and then all I could see was stars—but I did manage to get away," he concluded.

"I wasn't even in the wood, but it threw me from my bike," Ed began, "and I'm sure both of us could feel George's fear." He turned to June, who nodded.

"It was so painful; I tried to block it out, but it was everywhere, all around and inside my head."

"I felt paralysed, but not completely controlled," said Marcus, "and I couldn't release the stone when the orb called Carnyx commanded me to. It forced my arm to be outstretched, but I couldn't let go."

"I don't remember much," John admitted. "I can recall heading towards the Pogles Logs with Marcus, and I knew that George would be nearby. There were suddenly strobe lights leaping all around and I could see flashes of shapes, but they were like negatives from a roll of film. Then I was reaching out for the stone."

"And after June touched it, the second orb arrived," said Marcus.

"Yes, but we were forced into the wood to join you," said June. "I had no control over my legs, and there were really smooth, warm feelings inside my head."

"She's right," agreed George, "we were magnetised towards you; manipulated and soothed at the same time."

"If it can control us, why can't it just take the stone and leave us alone?" Ed complained.

"That's where the second orb—Thador—comes into the reckoning," Marcus suggested. "I think one's power may cancel the other's."

"If that's the case, then we should be free to do as we wish." June reached for a biscuit, cracking it and sending a shower of crumbs onto the carpet, which Shadow licked at lazily.

"What do you think they can do if we don't turn up tomorrow? After all, it is Christmas Eve—suppose some of us can't even come out?"

"I don't think we can doubt their power. They even stopped time tonight," Marcus replied. "And let's face it, if Thador hadn't arrived, there's no telling what might have happened. At least one orb appears to be on our side."

"Appears!" Ed exclaimed. "How can you contemplate trusting a weird, glowing sphere from goodness only knows where? What have we let ourselves in for?"

"Ed, we can only go on facts. What happened tonight was real. What happened to you and John the other night was also real," Marcus replied.

John agreed. "Like it or not, we seem to be involved in their power struggle. I think we should return tomorrow. After all, we have—or rather Marcus has—what they are after."

There was a silence which could have lasted for a minute or an hour, as they sat in a temporary trance, the sudden quiet ringing like wilderness in their ears.

"I'm puzzled by George's escape from the first

orb," June began.

"Yes," Ed interrupted, "how did you manage to run away?"

"I'm not sure," George admitted. "Perhaps the first orb didn't require my services!" He managed a half-smile.

"But we were all brought together—you were re-called," Marcus pointed out. "Even so, there must be a reason for it setting you free."

"It's all in the mind," June said jokingly, pointing at George's head. "They can control our brains—in his case, the first orb couldn't find one!"

"Actually, you might have a point." Marcus was serious.

"What do you mean?" said George indignantly.

"I mean, can you remember what you were thinking about immediately prior to disturbing Carnyx?" Marcus continued. "June's right, they can read and control our minds. It would be interesting if you can recall what Carnyx must have read."

George frowned. "Apart from the obvious curiosity as I approached the log, I don't know, really."

"Have a go, George. Think back," Ed encouraged him.

"Well...it might sound a bit silly," George began.

"Come on, of course it won't," said John.

"I was practising saying 'rhododendron' in Aigish in my head." George looked slightly embarrassed.

"That's it!" Marcus exclaimed. "That explains how you got away; it couldn't understand your thoughts."

Aigish was a coded version of the English language, once widely spoken by Horley's younger population, but now practised by only a few. Its use involved inserting "aig" in front of every sounding vowel, and the result, to an untrained ear or non-speaker, sounded like a confused nonsensical babble.

Marcus and George were the most proficient speakers in the group, and often held conversations completely in Aigish. Sometimes they would set each other difficult words to say—"rhododendron" being a prime example.

"If that's the case, surely a foreign language would confuse them too." June wondered if her knowledge of French would be of use.

"They're probably too intelligent to be confused by different languages for long." Ed was also wondering about using French.

"I think you're right," Marcus agreed. "Using a different language, or Aigish, probably puts up a barrier, until the pattern is recognised."

"You mean they could understand a new language that quickly?" George was intrigued.

"I'm just guessing, George. Assuming they have enormous intelligence, and that every language has its pattern, then yes."

"So, whatever happens tomorrow, we use Aigish

sparingly, right?" said John.

"Agreed." Marcus looked around at everyone. They had instinctively gathered closer, talking in hushed tones like a secret council discussing strange business, and formed into a circle for protection, as if huddled around an imaginary fire in the middle of the night.

"I'd better be going." June placed her empty mug on the tray and rose to her feet. "It's getting late and it's Christmas Eve tomorrow."

"Does anyone fancy going to Crawley in the morning?" Marcus asked as they all began to make a move.

"Talk about leaving your Christmas shopping until the last minute," Ed joked. "Alright, I'll join you. What time are you thinking of leaving?"

"About ten," Marcus replied. "Anyone else?"

George and John shook their heads.

"I've got relatives coming down from Birmingham," John explained.

"And I'm going to my brother's place for the day," said George.

"Marcus, you'd better set off earlier than ten o'clock." June couldn't believe him sometimes. "Everywhere will be absolutely jam-packed; remember, it's the last possible shopping day before Christmas!" She tutted under her breath.

"Looks like an early start then, Ed," Marcus looked at June sheepishly.

"I'll be round at 8:30," she said. "That way, we can be at the station by nine."

"I'll meet you there," said Ed.

George saw them to the door. "What time tomorrow night?" he asked.

"Better make it straight after tea," John suggested. "How about sixish?"

They all nodded.

"Shall we meet here?" Marcus shivered as he opened the door, and a rush of winter air slipped like a cold knife into the kitchen.

"Sure," George nodded. "Good luck until then."

They parted company after George had closed the door.

"See you in the morning!" Ed gave a short wave as he pedalled away.

June, who lived in-between George and Marcus, was soon indoors. She entered by the back door, where the kitchen window was steamed up as her mother prepared for the annual deluge of relatives. She headed for the lounge, curling up on the sofa in front of the TV, while her father grunted a muffled "Hello," in-between his newspaper and the roll-up cigarette which dangled precariously from his lip. June marvelled sometimes at how it appeared suspended, it seemed as if by magic, never dropping from her father's mouth while he puffed away, reaching for his petrol lighter every minute or so to reignite the stub.

Predictable Christmas entertainment floated before June's eyes as the TV chattered in the corner; more trailers than usual, as the station competed for its share of the prestigious festive season viewing figures, and more adverts for toys and games, which, by now, most parents could probably ill afford. June sighed, reflecting on the events of the evening, wondering what lay ahead.

Marcus and John paused momentarily in the driveway of Marcus's house.

"Well, John, you were right about something strange going on."

"Was I ever!" came the reply. "Give me a normal Christmas any day."

"We'll be OK, I know we will. See you tomorrow at George's."

Marcus turned and aimed for his own back door while John raced across the green to his house. Upstairs in his own room, Marcus placed the Stone on his table, then stood on the bed, looking out to the wood at the rear of Bolters Road. Through gaps in the clouds, stars peered down, and for a while, Orion the Hunter could be seen striding across the heavens.

The wood looked normal. Marcus rested his chin on the windowsill. "A normal Christmas," he sighed, thinking back to previous occasions, and one in particular when the family had raised their glasses at the dinner table. "Cheers!" The accompanying clink; arms aloft, "Merry Christmas!" as an ironic five flakes of snow fell like frozen tears into the garden. That was the closest it had been to a white Christmas since Marcus was eight.

On that Christmas Eve, the snow had come without warning, suddenly and silently like a ghost shedding its mantle. And Marcus and every other child had loved it; skidding down the street, making shapes, hurling snowballs, building lop-sided snow-men which froze the next night and gradually trickled away during the course of the next week.

On that Christmas morning, Marcus had dashed over to the pond in the closest field opposite the house with his Action Man: a soldier figurine which talked when the cord was pulled from its chest, barking a series of recorded messages.

*"Enemy in sight, range one thousssscchh—"* The end of that sentence was always cut short for some unknown reason. *"Commander to base, request support fire!" "Mortar attack, dig in!" "Action Man Patrol, fall in!"*

Marcus had taken the Action Man on its first mission to the icy pond, armed with its assortment of weapons and dressed in a green combat uniform topped with a plastic cap. Now it lay unused in its box inside the cabinet which rested on top of the wardrobe, suffering the fate of so many toys which were either outgrown or had lost their appeal. Then there had been the shooting range, which had remained in vogue for several months; a metal monstrosity decorated with targets and moving plastic ducks. This had been positioned at the front door and the would-be marksmen fired rubber darts from the end of the hallway. When the appeal of the shooting range had diminished, Marcus switched targets and took to ambushing his brother and sister.

He lay awake in bed for a while. The occasional car passed by in the street, pouring headlights into the bedroom which danced around the walls. He felt strangely secure in the darkness, although as a child, shadows had woven menacing shapes on the same walls; the shapes of contorted heads, or of bony fingers ready to snatch him away as he hid beneath the sheets, hardly daring to breathe and praying that his thumping heart would not give him away. Now there was no fear. Shapes on the walls could be explained as reflections or shadows thrown by various objects in the room. Soon Marcus was asleep, oblivious to his surroundings, while, on the side-table, the Stone changed colour, pulsating and emitting a thin sliver of light which stabbed forward into the darkness, rotating like a tiny searchlight.

In the wood, cloaked by midnight, Carnyx and Thador wrestled with each other's minds; resourceful, defending, challenging, searching for a weakness to exploit.

"You know that I have been sent to reclaim the

Balance, and it will be restored, Carnyx. These centuries have been peaceful. The only struggle has been caused by you and your kind."

"We grow restless, Thador. It is time for a change, and you know there is growing support in the Chamber for our ideals."

"Your ideals! The support comes only from others with evil intention. Peace and harmony will prevail. There will be no return to greed and holocaust. The Balance is our guide and you would only misuse its immense wisdom."

"You are an old fool, Thador. There will be no place for your kind."

Thador changed the subject. "What of Adam?" he asked.

"Adam was a fool," Carnyx replied. "He did not survive the journey back through time. At least we will not have to tolerate living human frailty any longer."

The two orbs were momentarily silent, for Adam had been the last with human form. When Eve had died childless, Adam had become deeply distressed and bitter at being so alone. And as the last with human form, he had abused his position to seize the Balance and use its power to time-travel.

Thador was saddened at the loss of his human comrade. "Human frailty is an inherent quality within us."

"It is no quality. It is weakness, and we despise weakness," Carnyx hissed, sensing Thador's sadness.

"Adam risked all to be with others of his kind. Of that I am sure," Thador responded.

"You naïve fool—do you think it to be a coincidence that Adam came back when he did? His appearance in this time was calculated to have maximum impact."

"What do you mean?" Thador was puzzled.

"Christmas! Are you so blind? Adam planned to return to this time as the New Messiah!"

"You are wrong, Carnyx. Adam would not abuse the Balance to such a degree."

"I know it to be true, for I followed his thought pattern. Adam was every bit as corrupt as you think me to be," Carnyx continued.

"As I *know* you to be." Thador was irritated. "And now what of the Balance? I am not here to bargain; I have come to claim what is rightfully ours."

"You repeat yourself, Thador. You are becoming old and forgetful. Nothing is rightfully yours."

"I may be older than you, but I am as strong as ever. You cannot overrule me. I can meet any challenge."

"Challenge? Yes, that will be the way. The old way. The Keeper will be set a challenge."

The two minds locked together once more, a temporary fusion of good and evil while the Earth yawned as morning approached.

# 8

# Christmas Eve

Marcus awoke early in the silvery half-light of winter dawn. Frost patterns pressed against the window, bathed by the feeble sun which gradually spread its brushstrokes further as it rose, like a golden bowl to be poured over the Earth.

The central heating was already on as Marcus peered down to the garden where birds pecked amongst the frozen blades of grass, puffed frills of feathers making them look bloated in the cold. From the clothesline, there hung a container of nuts, which attracted the more acrobatic birds who pecked hungrily in short, sharp movements. The weeping willow bowed gracefully by the iced-over pond, and there was not a stirring of wind.

By breakfast-time, half of the garden had thawed into sparkling droplets, while the other half remained locked in a vice of frost towards which the sun had not yet stretched. From the radio came the sound of familiar festive hits: John Lennon's *Happy*

*Xmas (War is Over),* and seasonal offerings from Slade and Wizzard as the DJ welcomed listeners to Christmas Eve.

Where Marcus sat, the sun became magnified by two windows so that it felt as warm and bright as summer. By 8:30, he was ready to leave the house—and June, punctual as always, knocked gently on the back door. "Are you ready yet?" she teased him.

"Of course I am," he replied in mock annoyance. "Mum, I'm off to Crawley," he began, as his mother commenced the ritual vacuum cleaning, the sound of which smothered speech and the music on the radio like a jumbo jet at take-off. Marcus shrugged and stepped outside. "It shouldn't take us long."

"You've got to be kidding!" June flicked her scarf at him as they laughed their way towards town. Already, there were people hurrying in all directions, and cars choking the roads with their exhaust fumes which hovered in acrid clouds at the junctions where queues formed. For many people, it was just another day at work. For the remainder, it was the time for last-minute shopping, and it seemed as though everyone had started early in an attempt to avoid one another. Marcus was glad of June's company, for he always found Christmas shopping an ordeal, and she always seemed to have ideas about which present would suit a particular person.

Being caught up in the early-morning movement

left little time to reflect on the encounter in the wood, nor their appointment later in the day. They reached the train station at five to nine.

"Hi!" Ed greeted them from the hard wooden bench at the side of the ticket office. "The next train is at twelve minutes past, and we have to change at Three Bridges."

Marcus tutted in exasperation, for even though it was a relatively short journey, it always involved the inconvenience of changing trains halfway. After buying tickets, they descended to the platform which was dark and cold and shielded from the sun, as traffic rumbled over the nearby bridge. To Marcus, a train journey somehow implied an outing, an adventure. It always seemed more of an occasion than taking the bus, notwithstanding the fact that the train conveyed you faster and further—about forty minutes up to London, or the same time in the opposite direction to the South Coast.

"How many presents are you buying?" Marcus asked Ed.

"Just a couple," he replied. "How about you?"

"Oh, just everything. Why do you think the expert is with me?"

June giggled as the Gatwick Express roared past on the opposite track, drowning the sound of her laughter, though her eyes were still smiling after it had passed, clattering and streamlined on its way to

London.

There was a surge of people towards the platform's edge, and soon the train pulled in, crammed full of shoppers and the last wave of workers on their way to Crawley. After threading their way through two full carriages, they retreated to a first class compartment where Marcus lowered the blind for privacy. At Gatwick Airport, there was a considerable wait. The public address system, which echoed and was muffled, seemed to confuse passengers on the platform who already appeared confused as they dragged luggage and children behind them. Then the train lurched forward. At Three Bridges, they sat in the graffiti-covered waiting room, where the only attempts at hiding the dubious witticisms had been to mask the more obviously offensive swear words. On every wall, there were scrawled or etched pledges to various football clubs and girls, together with other declarations of allegiance.

After a wait of ten minutes, the Crawley train arrived, crowded and with nowhere to sit. At Crawley station, almost everybody streamed out, ready to do battle, to jostle for position and to clog up the town. The shopping centre was a wriggling mass of people and, once caught up in the flow, it was extremely difficult to behave independently. In the clamour, recorded carols and messages boomed around the square, which was also full of rattling collection boxes and as-sorted Santas. It was difficult to communicate any intention, so Marcus pointed to one of the large stores and battled against a sea of bodies, while June grabbed hold of his jacket for support, and Ed followed through the heaving crowds. Once they were safely inside the store, the second major discomfort began, because the shops were always so hot and airless that it was necessary to remove the layers of winter clothing immediately, or else risk becoming cooked.

As they browsed, Marcus agreed eagerly to June's suggestions so that, before long, he had an armful of presents.

"You could probably buy that for less over the road," she said, pointing to the pot plant selected for Marcus's grandmother.

Marcus didn't reply. He was eager to make his purchases and then retreat from the madness.

Ed decided to go it alone. "Can we meet at McDonald's?" he asked, "say, in about an hour?"

"Sure, if we can all fit," Marcus replied.

"Well, OK, outside if there's no room inside," he said, and disappeared into another throng of shoppers.

Crawley was a vibrant and diverse place in which to shop, but although it was a "new town", it seemed to have aged and turned grey prematurely, he thought. The buildings were drab concrete and glass boxes, and the whole area seemed dour and colourless. And now, even with everywhere bursting with decorations, it still seemed lacking in soul somehow.

He slid his selections onto the checkout desk, and the barcode reader beeped in acknowledgement at each gift. All around was the hum of human conversation, all unintelligible in the roar of shoppers and cashiers.

They pushed their way out of the store, this time aiming for a record shop. In the centre of the square, the bandstand was host to a brass band which pumped an uplifting version of *Once in Royal David's City* over the heads of the gathered crowd. Within an hour, Marcus had finished his panic-buying, and they somehow found a spare table in McDonald's, where Ed soon joined them.

"How did you do, Ed?" June greeted him as he placed two carrier bags at his feet before sliding onto the bolted plastic seat.

"I'm finished for another year," he replied, reaching inside his jacket and placing a small box on the table.

"What's that?" Marcus asked. "Our Christmas present?" He nudged June, who promptly spilled a pile of chips.

"Clumsy!" she scolded him, and tried to snatch Marcus's fries away from him without success.

"Sort of," Ed shrugged. "I thought they might

come in handy—see for yourself."

June teased off the wrapping paper to reveal a wooden box which had a sliding lid. She gasped as the contents were revealed. "Where did you find these?"

"At the market. I couldn't resist buying them."

Marcus looked into the box in amazement, for there was a collection of shiny stones which so closely resembled the one which had made him the Keeper.

"It's incredible—surely they're not the same as mine?"

"I doubt it, Marcus; the stall-keeper had a whole box of them along with a load of cheap jewellery."

"These can't have come from the same place as yours," said June. "Let's see if we can tell the difference."

Marcus placed the Stone from Future Earth in front of them. In its present condition, the five that Ed had bought mirrored the original almost exactly.

"It's uncanny," said Marcus at length. "The only difference is that mine changes colour, especially when it's near the wood—although in London it resembled an ordinary pebble from the beach."

"I just thought they might be useful tonight." Ed placed them back in the box. "You know, as a kind of element of surprise. If not, we can always paint them brown and use them at school as fake conkers." He gave Marcus a wicked wink, picturing the champion conker of the season dangling from his wrist, unbeatable and completely plastic, or whatever material the stones were made from.

"They're a close enough copy, though I doubt they can fool our visitors. What exactly did you have in mind, Ed?"

"I'm not really sure," Ed admitted, "but, look, we don't know what might happen tonight. These might just be a form of insurance." He rattled the box.

"Let's share them out later. Maybe the orbs won't be able to tell the difference from the one they are after—and you know, Marcus, they couldn't take yours away." June's voice trailed off as fear of the unknown and the prospect of another encounter with the strange life forms emptied her mouth of speech.

Marcus instinctively felt her fear. "You're right, June. Even with the power they've demonstrated, neither Carnyx or Thador could take back what is so precious to them. It looks so small and unimportant," he continued, "and yet they call it the Balance, and me the Keeper."

"There's more to it than meets the eye." Ed pushed the Stone with his forefinger, and, just for a split second, had the feeling that he was being watched. By more than one pair of eyes.

# 9

# Future Earth

On Future Earth, the Chamber raged in crisis; the two sides of the Great Diamond Dome were in deep conflict as they received the thought patterns of their respective ambassadors, locked in mental battle, bargaining and negotiating ten thousand years in the past.

The walls of the Dome were cut and polished in the way of all diamonds. Sparkling, reflecting, and refracting the colours of the spectrum. Shimmering and spinning as the debate continued. On the Dark Side of the Chamber hung images of cruel, insane, and fanatical past leaders and despots, together with history's notorious murderers and perpetrators of other evil crimes. Beneath each image, there lay carefully preserved and maintained the respective thought patterns—all able to contribute to the Dark Side's bid to take control; seething, revolting and unspeakably evil; power denied the upper hand for centuries, and sensing an opportunity to seize it.

On the Light Side of the Chamber, the images were of the lovers of peace. Nobel Prize winners, artists, musicians, and scientists, together with their respective thought patterns, save for one—the image of a man which had no thought pattern beneath it. The image radiated beauty, calm, and purity. Suffering and redemption as his gentle eyes looked out over the Chamber. Serenely, sorrowfully, and with an enchanting demeanour despite the pain the image also represented. It was from here that the Balance had been stolen by Adam, the last human, and it was to here that it had to be returned for the Light Side to remain the Keepers. The representatives within the Chamber were orbs similar to Carnyx and Thador, all vying to contribute to the debate and the power struggle.

At the end of the Great Diamond Dome hovered the Master of Thoughts, who controlled the input to the debate, and at the centre of the vast floor, holographic images mirrored exactly the actions and conversations of five children on Earth ten thousand years in the past.

The debate was drawing to a conclusion. The Dark Side was last to contribute, with their claim on the ascent. From the thought pattern of one of the world's past leaders, there leapt a hologram which bristled and paced the floor, barking conditions and demands to the Light Side. A powerful and articulate orator with the complete support of the Dark Side. The image spoke in a strange tongue, which the Master of Thoughts automatically translated, and the speaker's last sentence, spoken in a shrill frenzy between clenched teeth, shrieked around the Chamber.

"It is time again!"

Then the image of the man clicked his boots, saluted the Dark Side, and was gone.

The Master of Thoughts gave the order of silence. "It has been decided, in consultation with our respective representatives in the past, that in accordance with the Old Ways, there is to be a Challenge set to the Temporary Keeper. The precise details of the Challenge are to be finalised by Carnyx and Thador, but they are to involve Ulah Ray. If the Challenge is not met, the Balance will be turned over to the Dark Side. To be successful, the human Marcus must return the Balance to the Light Side. Further details will be available from the Hologram Floor within the next orbit."

The Chamber darkened, and the two sides were momentarily respectful of each other. In accordance with the Old Ways, human frailty, ingenuity, cowardice, courage, love, hate, and all emotions would decide the Balance. It was the Law.

# 10

# The Challenge

They made their way back from Crawley by bus, boarding long before the mass exodus of late shoppers would clog every route leading from the town. They climbed to the upper deck, where the ride was bumpier, but gave a clearer view than the lower deck, which was filled with elderly people who chatted incessantly without really communicating, and young mothers who compared children, or struggled to control the exploring instincts of their offspring. The retreat of the upper deck was relatively calm in comparison, and Marcus was glad of the luxury of room in which to spread out his various purchases.

There were a multitude of dizzy roundabouts which the bus struggled to negotiate as it heaved and swung out in movements which were exaggerated to the upstairs travellers. At the Gatwick Straight, it picked up speed, rushing and rumbling beneath the airport which they had passed earlier in the day on the train. Minutes later, they swung into Horley's town centre, where Ed chose to depart.

"See you at George's." He waved as he negotiated the steep stairs. It seemed that they conspired to drag the unsuspecting passenger to the lower deck: even when you were sure the bus had stopped, it always seemed to make one final lurch which threatened to send you crashing downwards. And, of course, if you waited too long, it pulled away again, causing you to miss your stop. June and Marcus grinned as Ed fought to regain his balance.

"Mind how you go, Ed," June giggled. Marcus gave a short wave as Ed disappeared, then re-emerged on the street below as they pressed against the window to pull faces at him. Ed pointed up at them and made a face back.

Marcus and June rang the bell as the 405 neared the Chequers Hotel where they clambered off. Marcus's lower half was hidden by carrier bags as they struggled towards home. Although a sliver of sun still shone, the air was beginning to close around them. Slowly, the promise of a further frost whispered on the lips of approaching evening, and even though some two hours of daylight remained, there were still shaded areas where the ground had not thawed from the chill of the previous night. Their fingers were becoming numb by the time they turned into Kingsley Road.

"Shall we meet at George's, or do you want me to

call round for you?" Marcus asked.

"You'd better come round," June replied. "I might not be able to come out otherwise; you know what parents can be like at Christmas!"

"I know," he sympathised. "Still, we can say we're just going to George's for a while."

"I wish we really were."

Marcus comforted her like a big brother would. "It will all be fine, don't worry. And thanks for coming shopping. You don't want to help me wrap the presents, do you?"

"You...!" June protested. "Get on and do them yourself. I'll see you after tea!"

Once indoors, he went directly to his room to wrap the Christmas gifts—a task he could never quite master—and soon his attempts at wrapping littered the floor like strange origami. By the time Marcus had finished, the sun had sunk low in the sky, shredding the horizon with distant hues as Christmas Eve darkened and the stars began to click on one by one.

"Marcus!" his mother called him. "Tea's nearly ready."

He collected the presents and descended to the living room, where he placed them to join the existing pile at the foot of the moulting Christmas tree. His mother was drawing the curtains, always a sign of nightfall in summer or winter. He joined his brother and sister at the table, and ate in silence, unable to share in their obvious excitement and Christmas chatter, and speculation about what Santa might bring them. When the meal was finished, Marcus retreated to his room where he removed the Stone from his pocket once more, turning it over in his hands as one who held the key to a great mystery, yet could not find the lock in which it would turn. It was the colour of a blood orange, and as tough as diamond. Suddenly, Marcus was staring at the images of the two orbs, swirling and hovering in the wood.

"One hour, Marcus, and you will return." He recognised the command of Carnyx, followed by the gentle tones of Thador. "Have no fear, Marcus; be prepared and be true, for the future may depend upon you."

Marcus shook his head, blinking, and the images faded from the surface—or was it the vast depths?—of the Stone. And now, as he turned it, there appeared a shape beneath its surface. As he looked more closely, it seemed as if a small figure was attached to the shape. Marcus could make out an inscription at the foot of the image: A KISS IN TIME.

Puzzled, he continued to turn the stone; and now, into the picture there appeared an image of another man, and he was in a gallery: a hallway of breathtaking crystal, lined with pictures of people, some of whom he recognised as historical figures. The man was moving carefully and stealthily, cautiously looking around. At one particular image, he paused, before reaching towards a container at the foot of the figure. Then there was a flash, and the image flickered and was gone. A second later, another image appeared—this time, a page of blurred words which came gradually into focus as Marcus strained to decipher them. Headed A STAY OF EXECUTION, it read:

*The thought machine hums in rows and clicks, marching past my window.*
*The tall men pass with eyes like glass, reflecting my reflection.*
*The glint of knives in people's lives sharpens no illusion.*
*In dust awake and speed and shake, and add to my confusion.*
*And death could have saved me from all of this, washed like tears in the rain.*
*And if I come back, will they accept me, or sentence once again?*

*But if a stay of execution means another day for me,*
*I would cherish it like the treasure of possibility.*

*The leaps and bounds of murmured sounds, crushing all the flowers.*
*The tomb of doubt that falls about is locked in long lost towers*
*Which drip and moan and rot the bone by harsh and icy*

*friction;*
*And this is me, I'm still with me—*

*A voice without conviction.*

The page was signed:

*Adam.*

The Stone glowed and then dimmed like a bar cooling on an electric fire as the words faded. Marcus, suddenly aware that he had been holding his breath as he concentrated on the images, let it escape in a deep sigh. Ed's words earlier in the day were ringing with significance: "There's more to this than meets the eye." The enormity of the situation left no room for Christmas. He pocketed the Stone and decided to go round for June. It was not a time to be alone.

At six o'clock, they were assembled in George's room, tense and pensive.

"So we all received the message to be there in an hour?" John began. "I didn't think you'd believe it if it had been just me."

"Right now, I'd believe anything—especially after what Marcus told us about the Stone turning into a video screen," said George.

"Look, I can't be out for long. My mum thinks I'm just staying here," said June.

"Don't worry—I'm sure it won't be too late," Ed

comforted her. "Time to share out these," he said, placing the stones which he had purchased in Crawley on the carpet.

John and George looked at each other in amazement. "Where did you find those?" they asked in unison. Ed explained.

"There's one each," said Marcus.

"Show them how close they are to the real thing," June said.

"Here you are." Marcus reached for his stone to compare it with the others. As he leaned forward, it twisted between his fingers, slipping from his grasp, and tumbling into the stones below which scattered at the impact like skittles in a bowling alley.

"Oh, no!" he gasped. "Which is the real Stone?"

"Don't panic," said George. "Surely you can tell which one is which."

They gathered the stones together, and Marcus examined each one closely. They were all alike. "It's no good," he said in frustration. "They all look and feel the same."

"But yours is special; it must look different." June tried to console him.

"I don't know what might happen now. I feel like a prisoner awaiting sentence as it is." Marcus groaned.

"At least we know yours is one of the pile." George spoke calmly. "Why not take them all?"

"I guess I'll have to," Marcus sighed, "but that's

blown one of our ideas. Now we just have Aigish as a distraction."

"Are we all clear on that?" Ed asked. "We use it *sparingly*."

Everyone agreed. "Yes, if we want to be understood only amongst ourselves," Marcus concluded. "Time to go, then."

He scooped up the collection of six stones, which clinked and rattled in his pocket like marbles.

As they left the house, the first flakes of snow began to fall, lightly at first—but in the glow of the street light at the last house before the field, the snow could be seen to settle, and it tickled their faces as they walked closer to the wood.

Marcus led, selecting an entrance at the edge of the trees where he paused, looking back at the cosy houses opposite. A train on the track adjacent to the main road flashed electric blue as it travelled its icy rails—and how Marcus wished he were anywhere but here, on the brink of the unknown, preparing to step into something else. He turned and pushed into the wood.

"Come on, let's get this over and done with."

They gathered where they had stood the previous night, and the snow continued to smother the earth, its icy crystals saturating the air, and settling on the trees around them.

"Where are they?" June whispered.

"I don't know," Marcus whispered in reply.

Just as June began to hope the orbs would not return, a phosphorescent glimmer loomed in front of them, heralding the arrival of Carnyx and Thador, hovering closer, eerie in the icy whiteness reflected around them as the snow clung to branches and bushes, already hiding much of the ground. They stood in silent awe.

"You are wise to return," Thador spoke gently, and the children felt calmer. "It has been decided that, in accordance with the Old Ways, the Keeper is to be set a Challenge to decide the Balance." Marcus attempted to interrupt, but Thador continued: "He is to be taken to Hyeelthia, the domain of Ulah Ray, where the Dark Side has set tasks and challenges. These must be completed successfully in order for the Balance to be restored to the Light Side. Ultimately, the Balance is required to be returned to its place in the Chamber, within the Diamond Dome."

"But I don't understand," Marcus complained. "What are you trying to tell me?"

"Marcus," Carnyx hissed, "it is in your best interests to fail the challenge and return here to your friends. All will be well."

Marcus immediately knew that all would not be well, and he turned to Thador.

"The Balance was taken by Adam, the last human in our time, in order that he could time-travel to be with fellow humans. He arrived in your time, but did not survive the journey. The Balance has already displayed Adam's actions to you." Thador continued: "Carnyx and his kind will try to trick and corrupt you —that I cannot avoid—but you have my support together with that of the Light Side. Good shall prevail over evil. The Balance shall also protect you to a certain degree."

"Let us begin," Carnyx hissed impatiently.

"How will I know what to do? Who can I trust?" Marcus was desperate.

"You will know, young man, you will know, you will know..." Thador's voice echoed and then faded.

# 11

# Hyeelthia

There was a rush of air. A swirling expanse of oceans and space; of dimensions stretching and rebounding as the voice of Thador resonated and then disappeared. Marcus could feel his feet firmly on the ground, and yet he felt as though he was sinking and spinning downwards; flashing shapes leapt around as he sank into what appeared to be a huge box, its walls streaked with black and yellow racing past. And as he looked up, there was a reddish sky rapidly receding, and patterns flitted as though he were facing the sun on a summer's day, lying back in the grass with pressure applied to closed eyelids so that kaleidoscopic images bounced about.

"The Balance, show us the Balance!" A voice probed his numbed mind and Marcus reached for one of the stones in his pocket—and as he held it aloft, it was snatched from his grasp, whipped away like a bullet into the wind.

"Ha ha ha ha!" A devilish cackle drowned out the

rush of air. “The fool has failed already; see, I have the Balance!” The evil laughter echoed loudly—and then into Marcus’s field of vision came a bony talon clutching the stone which had just been ripped from his hand.

And then: “You tricked me!” a maniac’s voice screeched. “You foolish boy, you won’t do that again! You tricked me, and nobody does that twice.” And with a murderous wail, the voice receded, and the talon dropped the stone which shattered into dust; and Marcus continued downwards, slipping into unconsciousness. But before he became completely oblivious, a familiar, friendly voice soothed him.

“Marcus, we’re here. We’re not with you, but we’re here.” It was June comforting him. “We are able to guide you and to look over your shoulder.”

Her voice faded, and Marcus fell, powerless and without resistance through twisting tunnels, trembling and turning, effortless, onwards and downwards until he awoke in Hyeelthia.

At first, Marcus was unaware of his strange surroundings as he awoke gradually, his head slowly emptying as if from a deep sleep. But as he regained his senses, the nightmare memory of his strange journey returned—and his mind cleared and sharpened as he sat upright. Remembering the talon which had clutched one of the stones from his grasp, and the demonic laughter, Marcus searched in his pocket, and with relief felt the remaining stones—one of which was the Balance.

Wherever it was he had been taken to, the air was warm, moist, and gloomy, and the vision so poor that he instinctively placed his hands in front of him, shuffling forward on the sandy floor, aimless and blind in the strange void.

*"He is to be taken to Hyeelthia, the domain of Ulah Ray..."* Marcus recalled Thador's words.

On Future Earth, both sides of the Chamber watched in silence as the holographic image of a small human struck out across a barrier of darkness.

On Earth, John, Ed, June, and George were trapped in the snow and the wood, watching the same image projected onto the air in front of them.

"You are able to assist: each in turn may offer advice at each stage of the Challenge, and Marcus will hear you—but be clear, and do not confuse him with panic or irrational fear," Thador instructed them.

"And for my part, you will all feel what Marcus feels. It is an experience you will not forget," Carnyx promised.

"But how can we help? What are we expected to do?" June asked.

"Yes, we can't see any more than Marcus; it's completely dark," George insisted.

"Then help or you may suffer also. Think of the Light Side. More than this I cannot say." Thador offered a half explanation.

*"Think of the Light Side..."* Ed concentrated on Thador's suggestion, and as he turned the words over and over in his mind, they were repeated to Marcus in Hyeelthia, and he stopped in his tracks.

"Ed, I can hear you!" he exclaimed. "What do you mean?"

But there was no further communication, and Marcus's voice echoed cavernous against unseen walls. *"The Light Side?"* he thought, puzzled. *"Light, light..."* And in an instant, there was a flood of brightness that dazzled his eyes so that he had to shield them with his hands as he stood, blinking and exposed in a chamber carved, it seemed, from pure ebony. As his sight recovered and the glare became less painful, he reached out at the shiny wall which appeared to be right in front of him—and yet it was not. He turned around and marvelled at the uniformity of the chamber; smooth and flawless—and then above his head at a ceiling so high that it seemed to stretch forever upwards.

"Is anyone there?" His question rebounded, and the eventual silence was the only answer as he stood lost and alone. Gradually, the brightness began to fade, dimming like the lights in a cinema when the film is about to start, and Marcus began to panic, fearful of being swallowed once more by the claustrophobic cloak of darkness. And yet it did not return to pitch black, and overhead, he heard a flutter, barely audible, but there nevertheless. Looking upwards, Marcus was able to make out a thin beam of light which appeared to have no origin. The longer he looked at it, the closer to him it came until it formed an uninterrupted line stretching from high above down to the floor at his feet. As it did so, there was a swooping rush of air—and with a crackle, a piece of paper landed directly in the beam. Marcus reached for it, shaking dust from its surface which glittered as it tumbled to the sandy floor.

Headed HYEELTHIA, the document read:

*Deep, deep down where the darkness grows,*
*In a land full of dreams where it never snows,*
*Ulah Ray walks the chasm of time,*
*And inside his head is night's nursery rhyme—*

*To break all the children and shatter your smiles*
*In the turbulent tunnel which echoes for miles;*
*With his shield and his dagger, he limps for the souls*
*Who wait at night's window where nobody goes—*

*And checking the time that is always the same,*
*He mutters strange words, and he touches the mane*
*Of his fallen black sky-steed, the stallion of shadows*
*As it ploughs in the field by the orchard of crystal.*

*And when a horn blows in this underground world—*
*A signal that's felt but never quite heard—*
*The slaves of the cavern suspended are hung*
*From unseen ceilings which hide from the sun;*

*And Ulah Ray, in his dreams that are flung,*
*Beckons to you—and to him you must run.*

Marcus, who by now believed that anything strange which could happen probably would, was unable to understand the poem, which read like a riddle. He recognised Hyeelthia as the place to which he had been sent, and that it was the domain of Ulah Ray, but who on Earth was Ulah Ray?

In response to his thoughts, the same voice which had screamed so insanely during his descent echoed again: "On the moors of my mind at midnight we wait—ha ha! Seek the door into summer, or remain here forever—remain here forever, boy—ha ha!"

The sound swooped and dived and was carried away. "What is the door into summer?" Marcus asked aloud. The answer was his own echo followed by silence.

The light beam retracted, the room dipped further into darkness; and then, directly ahead, the wall began to pulse and to change hue, the colours of the spectrum inviting him to draw nearer. Attracted by the various shades, Marcus approached. At a distance he judged to be a metre from the wall—which now alternated in colour between crimson and violet—there appeared four doors, and above them a large inscription carved in ancient stone: A DOOR FOR EACH SEASON.

George's voice crackled in Marcus's ear. "One of us is allowed to offer advice at each stage of the Challenge," he explained. "It's my turn," he continued. "We can see and feel what is happening, Marcus—be careful. You have to pick the door into summer at this stage to continue. There must be a clue somewhere, but hurry—you are trapped in Ulah Ray's mind; we think you are in Hell and that he is the Devil!"

Marcus gasped. "Help me choose, George, get me out of here!" George was unable to reply, and Marcus was alone again, but watched by distant audiences; the viewers on Earth were also involuntary participants.

Each door, on first inspection, looked identical, veiled by a silky material, and made of pure white marble. Each had a knocker at the centre. He re-read the Hyeelthia poem, hoping for an answer to the four door puzzle. *"And inside his head is night's nursery rhyme..."* It seemed significant in the light of the suggestion that he was trapped in Ulah Ray's mind—that of the invisible madman—so, presumably, he shared the same mind as that containing night's nursery rhyme. *"Was that a clue?"* he wondered, trying to recall the childhood songs and rhymes passed on by his parents in his formative years. Frustrated, he drew a blank, unable to remember any references to night's nursery rhyme. Marcus reached for the five remaining stones.

"Please help me choose," he pleaded. "Which is the real Stone?" They clinked together in the palm of his hand as he turned them over, searching desperately for one that appeared unique—searching desperately, but in vain.

He approached the first door again, peeling back the veil so that it draped over his head and shoulders. It was pure white, icy, and smooth-glazed, unmarked, perfect. The knocker was made of brass, and Marcus lifted it, curious to know what the door might reveal if he knocked upon it; and there, hidden by the heavy brass ring, was a tiny picture: so small it was difficult to make out. He went down on his knees, and peered closer at what resembled a man shaped like an egg, perched precariously on a wall. Of course, he recognised it—Humpty Dumpty! He carefully replaced the knocker and moved on to the second door, wondering if this was a clue...but what if all the doors had hidden pictures of Humpty Dumpty? What if none of them had? It also occurred to him that, if the doors represented the seasons sequentially, the door into summer should be the second. He examined it in the same way as the first.

He removed the veil, and crouched level with the knocker, which he lifted to reveal a picture of Little Bo Peep. At least the nursery rhyme theme was proving consistent. Onto the third door, and here was a picture of a grey-haired old man, dressed in a white gown, clutching a candle glowing in its holder. Puzzled by this image, he moved to the fourth and final door which revealed a black sheep with three bags at its side: of course, Baa, Baa, Black Sheep. Was the colour of the sheep a reference to night in the Hyeelthia rhyme? Marcus could not be sure—and why, in any case, have darkness as a reference to a door into summer? And then Marcus began to realise the significance of the man depicted on the third door: surely that was a character running through the night, checking to make sure the children were tucked up safely in their beds.

Suddenly the menacing voice interrupted his thoughts. "A decision, Marcus!" it screamed hysterically. "Choose now, or lose the Balance. I'm waiting..." To emphasise the point, a loud ticking like that of an enormous clock began.

"Please let me have made the right choice." He spoke aloud as he brushed aside the veil of the third door, carefully lifting the knocker, slowly and agonisingly, until the decision was irreversible. He brought it down sharply, once, twice, three times, grimacing as he did, each knock sharp and incisive.

And now there was silence, save for the ticking which continued as before. Marcus stepped back, almost sure that he had chosen the wrong door.

"What do I do now?" He began to panic, and then there was a cacophony of a million bells; an enormous cathedral clanging which caused him to jump, startled. The noise was intense and engulfing, and he was suddenly aware of the need to escape its deafening tremors. Marcus pushed at the door which was as solid as it appeared. Annoyed and afraid, he took a small run-up at it, and heaved with all the effort he could summon—and with increasing desperation, he approached it a third time, and it opened before he could stop himself from passing through.

# 12

# The Feast of Running Tide

Marcus tumbled with arms outstretched to break his fall, which was cushioned by a large tuft of grass. He had landed in a forest, leafy and verdant, with soft emerald light trickling through the trees. Birds twitched and twittered on branches. Warmth wrapped around him from a saffron sun. Marcus looked back for the door, but it had vanished. He rose to his feet, confused but grateful for a more familiar environment—in fact, anything within reason would have been better than enduring the blasting he had received from the alarm bell; and surely his arrival here meant that he had chosen correctly. *"The door into summer,"* he thought. *"Perhaps I can go home now. Maybe the challenge is over."* And in the comfort of the warm day, he wondered about Christmas Eve, and whether he had yet been missed. Surely, if anyone came looking, they would not find him here. And then what of John, Ed, June, and George—where were they, and how could they communicate every so often?

Back in the wood, trapped in time, the four friends received Marcus's thoughts.

"Shall we reassure him?" June asked. "He seems confused."

"Of course you should," Carnyx agreed. "He needs periodic contact."

Thador cut in. "Choose your moment of communication carefully," he advised. "There is only one opportunity at each stage, so use it wisely. Do not be tempted by this dark soul."

"Thador is right," John agreed. "It's my turn next; let's wait and see what happens."

Isolated in the wood, the children and the orbs were invisible. They were cloaked by dimension-sharing, and insulated from outside interference, surrounded by the still-falling flakes of snow; and yet strangely warm inside the invisible Glimmersphere which hid them while the challenge progressed.

"Perhaps we should concentrate on the Hyeelthia rhyme," Ed suggested, "Thador, can we ask you for any help?"

"I can only advise that any helpful clues contained within the verse have been concealed, at least in part, by the Dark Side. It would be unsafe to assume too much and place any credence on the rhyme in its entirety."

"You may take it as the blueprint for the Challenge," Carnyx countered. "Trust me."

Marcus shuddered in the sunshine as the words spoken by Carnyx overlapped dimensions, causing him to feel a wave of revulsion as he recognised the evil intent. He began to steer a course through the forest, directionless but possessed with a purpose to discover his whereabouts. For a while he continued unhindered, but gradually the undergrowth became thicker, and it wasn't until his arms and legs were lashed by the first thorn bushes that Marcus realised he was not wearing his normal clothes. Gone were the familiar jeans, trainers, T-shirt and cardigan which he had been wearing under his winter coat, to be replaced by crude clothing made from animal fur, of two types, he guessed, for it was part grey and part brown, and there was a rough string intertwined with shreds of leather which ran up across his shoulder and down his back like a half brace. His feet were also covered with furs which served as primitive boots, tied on with the same crude string which ran across his upper half.

*"So where's the fancy dress party?"* he wondered, reaching for a stick with which to beat a path forward. *"There's no point in turning back,"* he convinced himself. As the forest became more dense, so the sunlight became less concentrated as it was trapped and filtered by the increasing foliage. Marcus began to perspire as he eased further. After ten minutes of

exertion, he burst into a clearing where rabbits, leaping and twitching in the sunlight, were startled; and, beating the thump-thump of a warning, quickly retreated from view. Stumbling across the clearing had come as a pleasant surprise, and, for the first time since the start of the Challenge, Marcus was aware of a growing hunger and thirst. He was also aware of another presence—one which he could not define, but which made him feel uneasy, and at once uncomfortable. He paused in the middle of the clearing and concentrated, listening intently. All appeared calm, birds filling the air with song, then a slight hush, and the rustle of light wind billowing in the trees. White butterflies danced across the ground in noiseless fluttering ivory movements, followed by the heavy snap of a twig. And it was then that the birds stopped singing.

Marcus continued his route across the clumps of grass, away from the sound of the snap. But instinct or sixth sense caused him to turn back before he had reached the start of the forest on the other side, and, whirling around, he was faced with the sight of a huge brown bear lumbering from the undergrowth. It raised its head and roared menacingly as he broke into a run. Fortunately, the forest was less dense on this side, and Marcus leapt and sped his way around roots, bushes and vegetation, spurred on by the sound of the bear crashing through the forest, right on his trail. He imagined it gaining on him, its claws raised, ready to shred his flesh—and in his haste, he tripped on an exposed tree root which sent him hurtling and uncontrolled down a steep incline where he rolled over brambles and nettles, cursing his loss of balance, scrambling uselessly to grip at something that would halt his descent. The tumble knocked him breathless, and as he shook himself clear of the tentacles of undergrowth, the bear reached the crest of the incline, and continued to lumber down towards him, relentless and hungry. As Marcus backed away, the bear rose on its haunches and bellowed at him terrifyingly.

"Get up that tree!" John yelled at him. "Move it, Marcus! It's closing in on you, come on!"

With legs leaden with fear, Marcus responded. Immediately to his left was a leafy elm which offered a safe haven, but only if he could climb high enough in time. He jumped at the lowest branch, hung agonisingly in the air, and fell uselessly to the ground. This seemed to encourage the bear further, and it quickened its rate of approach. Marcus lunged at the branch, and used his body momentum to swing so that he was able to pull himself up, resting on the branch with his arms locked and body taut. As he hauled himself up, the bear charged at the tree, roaring in anger as Marcus swung out of reach. It clawed at the bark, slashing it so that sap oozed and dripped from the deep cuts. It rose to its full height, and continued to roar menacingly while Marcus clung to a branch some three metres above the bear's highest reach, shaking uncontrollably and wondering, miserably, how to escape from this predicament. The bear circled the tree, scraping at the ground and nuzzling at the bark. Then it rose once more, sniffing the air as though sampling a delicate bouquet.

There was a sudden twang followed by a slapping sound, and the bear roared again, this time more fiercely than before, though not sustained. Marcus peered downwards through the soft green leaves of the elm, and saw the bear writhing at the foot of the tree. It rolled over—and now he could see the shaft of an arrow protruding from its chest, and the bear was bellowing painfully, scrabbling at the deeply embedded missile. It rolled again, pushing the arrow shaft still further, and Marcus could hear its breathing: strained and shallow, slipping away. He felt the whole tree tremble as it careered into the trunk; and then it staggered weakly in short zig-zags before rolling over. It wheezed and then fell silent. And when it had breathed its last, a small hairy man strode confidently forward, wielding a bow with arrows strapped at his waist, with a leather shield at his side, and dressed in the same style of clothing as Marcus. The man looked up at Marcus, tossed back his mane of black hair, and gave a huge throaty laugh. He threw back his head, and laughed again and again with eyes like obsidian twinkling, while Marcus continued to stare in amazement at the strange hunter who had saved him from the bear.

When his laughter had subsided, the man approached the tall elm and shouted out, "Marcus, small one, you had better come down now. The Feast of Running Tide nears." And then more seriously: "What do you think you are doing roaming the Great Forest unarmed, you fool? Even Old Woman the Berry Picker would be a better match for a bear." He scowled and spat in the direction of the lifeless animal. "And how am I to carry this back to the village with only your help?" he continued.

Marcus, who felt like asking a thousand questions, thought better of it, and scrambled down. "I got lost. I'm sorry," he apologised.

"Then it is just as well that Mythanee the Hunter knows when his son is in trouble. Praise be to the Old Ones." He raised his fist aloft, then pulled it to his chest. Marcus did the same, and Mythanee the Hunter seemed satisfied at the gesture. "Her mate will be wild with anger and after us if we're not quick," he said; and, with an incredible turn of strength for a man of such small stature, he stooped and heaved the bear onto his shoulders where it bounced and bobbed as they walked in silence. Marcus marvelled at the man's speed with such a load; he threaded his way tirelessly, twisting and turning, and then joining a trail which appeared well used, until they reached a small valley which had a path of sand leading down. The air smelled of salt, and when Marcus looked further ahead, the ocean rose to meet the sky, and the two elements appeared as one. The clouds hovered like the far-away mountains of an undiscovered land as they descended into the valley where faint wisps of smoke rose, and soon Marcus could make out small round huts from where the smoke spilled into the early evening.

As they neared the small mud-hut village, an atmosphere of activity and expectation could be felt, and Mythanee quickened his step so that Marcus had difficulty in matching his pace. "Come on, boy!" he encouraged him. "The night draws near, and soon it will be time to light the beacon on the hill." He nodded in the direction of the opposite side of the valley, the side closest to the ocean, where a small army of women laboured to raise logs and branches to add to a huge pile of firewood at the top of the hill.

When they neared the first hut, from an opening draped with animal hide there emerged a large man clothed in strips of fur, his skin coarse and grained with mud, eyes red and sore from the smoking fire inside his mud dwelling. He greeted Mythanee with an approving grunt as he marvelled at the sight of the great bear.

“You have done well, Mythanee the Hunter. The Feast of Running Tide shall be even more magnificent.”

Mythanee drew level with the man, staring fiercely into his grizzled face; and then he laughed just as he had done at Marcus while he had trembled in the tree. With his head thrown back, he rested it against the belly of the bear, exposing the blackened stumps of his rotting teeth. At first the other man appeared intimidated, but gradually he too joined in the laughter, slapping his great belly so that the folds of flesh quivered underneath his furs.

“Praise be to the Old Ones!” the man cried, making the sign with his hand and then drawing his arm to his chest.

“Praise be indeed, Great Belly.” The Hunter returned the sign, and continued forward with Marcus a pace behind, squelching in the mud. There were about twenty equally spaced huts in the settlement, at the nucleus of which were two larger units.

Most of the adults they passed were preoccupied in tasks such as animal-skinning and arrow-making, but a few children scampered at their heels excitedly, voicing their approval at the sight of the bear.

At the first of the large huts, Mythanee halted, dropping the dead weight from his shoulders so that it thudded to the ground.

“I have returned, Eva—and see here, your foolish

son is unharmed!" He cuffed Marcus, though not unkindly. From the skin-screened entrance, a woman's face appeared, smiling a welcome—and with delight twinkling in her eyes when she saw what her husband, the Hunter, had brought from the forest. She emerged from the hut to greet them.

"This will indeed please the Old Ones," she said softly, her golden hair enhanced and highlighted in the weakening sun.

"All is ready," she continued. "The beacon is built." She nodded in the direction of the great hill where the women of the village had completed their task. Eva turned to Marcus. "The Feast starts at sunset. Eat your fill, Marcus, for your journey will be long and arduous."

He decided it was best to continue to play along, for it seemed he was accepted within the village, and was acknowledged as their son. The idea of a feast was appealing; he was becoming ravenous, and yet he was puzzled by the continuation of this aspect of the challenge. Surely his encounter with the bear had been settled with Mythanee's archery skills. Why, then, continue in this theme if the bear was slain? With a start, Marcus thought of the stones, and, clutching at his sides, felt with relief their familiar rattle, for they were safely stored in a small leather pouch which was strapped to his thigh.

He was ushered into the hut which was surprisingly spacious. The floor was lined with straw, and there were what he guessed to be crude beds fashioned from fur and cloth, positioned close to a fire which burned in the middle. Although there was a hole in the roof directly above for the smoke to escape, most of it hung in a haze, permeating the entire room and causing Marcus's eyes to sting. Eva turned her attention to a dark pot suspended in the flames. She stirred it and sipped from it, mumbling words which were unfamiliar to Marcus, while Mythanee chipped away at flints to produce arrowheads. With a sigh, Marcus chose a position in the straw near a wall, which he noticed was adorned with bones embedded in the mud. One in particular made him shudder, for he recognised it to be a human skull. Eva's strange chanting had a comforting effect, and soon Marcus became drowsy, his head slowly drooping, eyelids closing, the fire warm and soporific, the tap-tap of stone on stone. He soon sank into a deep slumber.

When Marcus awoke, he was alone, and the fire had reduced to a heap of grey, smouldering ash. He was cold and stiff from sleeping uncovered on the floor, and he reached for one of the nearby furs. He sniffed at it distastefully before picking up a blanket which was as rough as a coal sack, harsh and itchy—though it smelled clean, and was warm. He parted the covering at the entrance to the hut, and peered out. Night had fallen; and upon the hill, a huge fire had been lit. It was so huge that it reminded him of Bonfire Night. The occupants of the village were making their way towards the hill, carrying torches to guide them. Marcus could pick out the figures climbing the hill like a long line of slowly moving fairy lights strung out over the valley. Eva startled him as he stared at the procession.

"It is time," she said simply. "Come now, for the Feast awaits you."

At the thought of nourishment, he scrambled from the hut, and, with Eva, joined the procession. Halfway up the hill, the heat from the huge fire could already be felt, and when they had reached the crest, some fifty or so villagers were gathered around smaller fires, where pots bubbled and steamed, and meat roasted on spits. Nearer to the beacon, which sent sparks and flames heaven-bound as it roared and crackled, there had been etched a line: and along its length, there had been placed an array of furs, weaponry, carvings, and metalwork. The villagers at the head of the procession each walked forward in turn to the line to add to the assortment. Marcus could see that Eva carried nothing—and, as he wondered where Mythanee could be, a drum began to beat, and the Hunter stepped from a circle of villagers. He was draped with the head and fur of the skinned bear which he had felled earlier that day. Eva pushed Marcus towards him, and Mythanee growled menacingly, imitating the creature whose skin he now wore. He motioned Marcus towards the circle from which he had broken, and it was then that Marcus realised the men and women had formed separate circles surrounding different fires. The drum beat continued, gradually but noticeably quickening like a speeding heart; and the men in the circle began to chant:

*"Feast of Running Tide, the Old Ones on the hill. Bathed in beacon light, for warmth against the chill."*

The chant quickened, and the words began to race together, whining, nasal, feverish—until there was a last thump of the drum. And then the circle fell silent.

Mythanee stood slowly, and all eyes were on him. "Let the feast begin," he commanded, "and let no man move from the circle until the time has come." The drum began to beat again, and the women of the village moved among the men, offering food and wine which was snatched greedily and consumed noisily, with spent bones raining down on the fire as night-time began to fade into day.

Marcus ate his fill and began to grow weary again, and, just as he began to lower his head with fatigue, Mythanee the Hunter rose to his feet, throwing the bear skin to the ground and clapping his hands.

"It is time!" he cried, with arms held aloft. "Sunstar nears. The Old Ones must have their Feast, for they are all-consuming. Praise be to the Old Ones." He made the strange sign, and the whole village copied the salute.

"And now Marcus—son of Mythanee and Eva—begins his journey as the Old Ones have decreed." The Hunter moved towards Marcus, and thrust a shield and dagger into his grasp. Another chant began, and this time the women joined in. At first Marcus could not understand, until, to his utter amazement, he recognised the use of Aigish. They were chanting in the secret language of his own childhood, and the words referred to the great fire which still raged, blazing as dawn broke and the sky yielded colour.

*"Into the beacon, into the beacon."*

And now the true horror of the situation became evident, for it was intended to offer him as a sacrifice to the Old Ones. The men and women of the village were now in formation, edging him closer to the beacon, chanting and trance-like until he was trapped. Surrounded by them as they formed a circle around him and the fire. And then the circle began to tighten, moving closer, squeezing towards Marcus, villagers dropping from it as the remainder relinked, pressing forward relentlessly.

In desperation, he sought a gap, lunging and preparing to use the dagger in an attempt to escape. But the heat was intense and his vision blurred. The chant increased in volume.

*"Into the beacon, into the beacon!"*

Everywhere he turned, there was heat and madness as he was forced closer still to the furnace. With hair singed and smouldering now, with skin prickling and the shield raised to protect his face, he turned to look at his tormentors. As he did so, there was an angry roar of crackling timber, and a leaping of fire-tongued lashing flames as the all-consuming furnace collapsed and smothered him.

Flames flickered in front of his eyes, although he was sure they were closed. In the deafening molten crash and searing heat, the chanting faded. Marcus felt as though he was descending again, carried away by the flames which licked at him without burning. And now they were as green as emerald: icy, soothing, and caressing his skin. As cool as the feel of an ocean-deep pearl. Cold crystal comfort, satin wrapped around him, turning and smoothing until he felt no more. Washed like tears in the rain.

# 13

# Moonchild

On a strange shore, Marcus sat with head cradled in his hands, silent after his ordeal in the flames. The air was saturated with sodium above the salt-baked shore, streaking his hair white while the sea unfurled, lashing dripping rocks at the water's edge. The ocean raced up towards him, with foam filtering through the sand like a negative eclipse. He felt a madness in the salty clamour and roar of the hungry ocean, and the tinted distance of an unknown horizon made him feel insecure and insignificant. At his side lay the shield and dagger, and, fluttering in the breeze, the Hyeelthia poem. Its flapping annoyed him, and he snatched it from the bed of red pebbles. It was then that he noticed the first six lines of the rhyme had disappeared.

There descended a chill, followed by a ghostly calm. Then, rolling from the sea, a mist seeped towards him with wisps of vapour rising. The already faint light faded further, so that the only illumination came bleak and cold from the swirling ocean mist. Marcus reached for the shield and dagger, and rose to his feet, moving forward on pebbles awkward to tread, crossing the path of dark where broken rocks, jagged and crimson, tumbled to the edge of the swell. And he waited expectantly.

Ed wiped beads of perspiration from his brow. "That was a close call. I didn't think he'd make it," he exclaimed.

"I could feel everything," June agreed. "The panic, the confusion."

"And most of all, the heat," John added.

In the Glimmersphere, they watched as Marcus made his way cautiously to the water's edge.

"You are permitted contact before the next stage of the Challenge," Thador informed them.

"How much more must Marcus endure?" George protested.

"Come now, the Challenge has barely begun, and I assure you no harm will come to him," Thador replied.

"The Challenge will be over the moment he fails," Carnyx interrupted.

"He won't fail." June was defiant. "Let us talk to him now."

"In turn, then," Thador agreed.

George spoke. "Marcus, can you hear me? We are with you. We know you can do it."

Marcus stood alone on the brink, unwavering as the water lapped at his feet, concentrating on nothing, waiting.

"He hears, but will not respond. He is adjusting to the Challenge," Thador explained.

"Such resilience and resourcefulness for one so young," Carnyx said impatiently, "though surely he is doomed to failure. Ulah Ray will see to that."

And as Carnyx uttered his words of gloom and dark despair, one of the stones fell from Marcus's pocket and rolled into the velvet ocean. For the second time, the words of Carnyx twisted through time and dimensions to repeat in Marcus's ears, and he stirred from his trance.

Gliding towards him through the misty salty air was a ghostly shape; silently approaching, cutting a tunnel like a black comet as it grew nearer. Marcus was not afraid. He held the leather shield in his left hand and clutched it to his chest. The dagger, jewel-encrusted and sparkling, was in his right hand as the apparition neared noiselessly. It was a girl, pure and beautiful, hair flowing like soft gold dripping, draped in pristine whiteness with eyes like drowning sapphires—and she held out her arms in a greeting.

"Hello, who are you?" he asked.

The girl advanced no further. She looked at him with a smile soft and sweet like rubies in the snow, perfect yet cold.

"I am known as Moonchild," she replied gently, still smiling at him, "and I have come to you, for you waited for me."

"I didn't know..." he began.

"Hush, now," she raised a finger to her lips. "You have waited for me upon the shore, at night's window where nobody goes."

"I don't understand," he said.

"Oh, but you do, Marcus, you do. And now your gifts, please," she spoke more firmly now. "To continue, you must let me have the gifts."

Marcus shrugged. "If you mean these, then you're welcome to them." He held out the shield and dagger, and she took them from him.

"This will please the Light Side." Moonchild smiled again. "His shield and dagger, such power for the Balance. You have done well, Marcus. You may continue."

"But where? Where must I go now?" he asked.

She placed a finger to her lips once more. "Hush, I must go now." Then she receded, slowly at first, face upward turned, voice fading to a whisper. "Sink or swim, but see where the moon swirls upon the water. Jump there, and you will be saved. Life is like porcelain..."

The sea mist enveloped him, claustrophobic, clinging to his hair and eyelashes as the sound of the waves tumbling to the shore changed. It was still the sound of water, and the saltiness of the air remained, but the ground felt smoother, and it tilted slightly but noticeably.

# 14

# Futility

As the shroud of the mist cleared, Marcus found himself staring out to sea. He was standing on the deck of a ship. He moved towards the handrail, and gasped at the enormous drop beneath to the ocean. The deck was almost deserted. There were a couple of people to his left leaning against the rail, also looking out to sea, and a few reclining in deck-chairs, almost hidden as they huddled against the cold, and far above his head stretched a row of four huge funnels which sent smoke billowing sideways as the ship progressed.

Just looking at the closest funnel made him feel giddy, and he turned away. As he did so, there was a shout and stream of excited laughter. "Marcus!" He heard a cry, and towards him ran a girl, dressed in a full-length cream coloured dress, her hair in ponytails which danced and shook in the sea breeze as she ran towards him, her black shoes clipping the deck like a trotting horse.

"Marcus!" she exclaimed breathlessly, "I've found you—even on the largest ship in the world, I've found you! I looked everywhere, but didn't expect to find you right up here in the cold. Aunt Emily is on the promenade deck below. We should rejoin her; it's much warmer with the glass to protect us from the cold—come on!"

He judged her to be a couple of years his junior, and, before he could respond to her bubbly enthusiasm, she had gripped his hand and begun to lead him away, skipping in the cold sunshine, tugging at him, and imploring him to move more quickly. "Come on, slow coach!" she giggled.

They entered the enclosed section of the deck, and descended a staircase which led to an area like a foyer, carpeted and marked FIRST CLASS ENTRANCE—FIRST CLASS PASSENGERS ONLY. Still leading him by the hand, the girl pulled him through another door and out onto a deck again. Yet this was shielded from the cold by glass, so that the sunlight streamed onto them like a bright cascading waterfall of sunbeams.

"Aunt Emily, I've found him!" she cried triumphantly, propelling Marcus towards a rather serious-looking woman clad in a dark, full-length dress. She was reclined in a wicker chair, sipping delicately from a finely balanced cup and saucer.

"So you have," the woman replied. "Marcus, your sister is becoming too clever for you. Karen, sit down and conserve some energy; and, Marcus, please go to our rooms and fetch my book and reading glasses." She thrust a door-key into his hand, motioning for him to leave as she returned her attention to her China tea and the panoramic view of the sweeping ocean.

Marcus re-entered the foyer by the same door through which Karen had led him, and he stopped to examine the key which had the number B47 engraved upon it.

"Can I help you, young sir?" An immaculately dressed crew member approached him. "Lost, are we, sir?"

"Well, yes, I..." Marcus mumbled.

"Ah, yes, sir—B47. This way, if you please." The officer led him down a richly carpeted corridor. Its walls were lined with walnut, and there was a row of softly glowing lamps. At cabin B47, the officer paused, turned the key in the lock, and swung the door open to allow Marcus inside.

"Good day to you, sir." The man turned on his heels and disappeared back along the corridor.

Marcus marvelled at the ornately decorated cabin. The walls were wood-panelled, as was the ceiling, which was intricately patterned, and had a large light-shade at its centre which hung like an upturned glass bowl. There were a number of chairs, a luxurious bed in the corner of the room, and a small side-table.

There was a side door in the cabin, and Marcus walked through to a similarly appointed twin berth which he imagined belonged to his Aunt Emily and sister Karen. On the side-table was a neatly placed, thin, leather-bound book titled *Futility* by Morgan Robertson, and a pair of glasses which he collected. On the opposite side of the cabin, on another side-table, stood a small statue of a unicorn, white and fragile, with the inscription PRANCER beneath it. Just as Marcus turned to leave the room, his curiosity was aroused by what appeared to be a newspaper protruding slightly from underneath one of the beds. He walked over, and pulled it from the recess. It was a crumpled copy of the Daily Mirror dated 10th April 1912.

He replaced the paper, and turned to leave, locking the outside door, and retracing his steps to the foyer and the door which led to the Promenade Deck. The deck was still steeped in sunshine, and Marcus rejoined his unfamiliar relatives, placing the book and glasses on the table in front of Aunt Emily.

"Now, you may go exploring with Karen—but mind you are back here and ready for lunch by midday, Marcus. And do not speak to any other passengers unless they speak to you. Oh, and Marcus," she added, "on no account are you to stray from the First Class areas of the ship. I will not tolerate you mixing with Second Class or Steerage passengers."

There was a moment's awkward silence. "Is that understood?" The woman raised her voice, slightly annoyed at his lack of response.

"Yes, Aunt Emily," he replied.

"Very well, then. Off you both go."

"This way, Marcus!" Karen sprang to her feet, and set off in the opposite direction.

"Don't run, Karen," her aunt scolded as Marcus struggled to keep up with the exuberant girl. At the end of the glass screening was a sign which read SECOND CLASS—PROMENADE.

"Hold on, Karen; we can't go any further this way." Marcus drew level, and this time he took her hand. "Look, there's another doorway here; let's try it." They stepped into another foyer which contained a staircase similar to the one they had taken earlier. They descended to the next deck; and around the stairwell, the dull mechanical chug of murmuring machinery could be heard, the very heart and soul of the ship talking to them through thick engine room casing.

Karen's eyes, wide as saucers, gleamed. "Wow, Marcus, listen. I can hear the ship's heartbeat!"

"That's because we're lower; we're a deck nearer to the engine room," he explained. They walked into another foyer where people strolled surely and easily, formally dressed yet relaxed. Men escorting their wives, with polite exchanges taking place as first class passengers passed each other. Marcus marvelled at the mirror images the children reflected of their parents, for they were dressed as miniature adults, and seemed strictly controlled. At the first turn they made, there was a barber's shop where a row of severe-looking men sat in various stages of their morning shave.

"Don't they look serious?" Karen giggled, pointing at one elderly gentleman who sported a heavy, drooping moustache which twitched when he spoke; words which were inaudible to them, but which no doubt conveyed instructions to the barber as he prepared to scrape another wealthy chin.

They continued along the corridor, joining the gentle flow of people, passing cabins, bathrooms, and a room marked STEWARDS, until they reached the final door on the left: the Sitting Room—which they entered. It was unoccupied, and Marcus wondered why so much effort had been made to make the room look as unshiplike as possible. Apart from an occasional soft roll underfoot, it was difficult to believe they were at sea. The décor was as immaculate as the cabins; walls carved and decorated with coving tracing the expanse of ceiling, a Georgian sofa and chairs, and even a mock bay window with curtains neatly drawn and tied at the bottom.

"What shall we do in New York?" Karen asked him. "I've been so looking forward to going there, but I wish our journey could last forever."

"New York?" Marcus said vaguely. "I suppose it might as well be there as anywhere."

"What do you mean? You've been looking forward to the trip just as much as I have. Come on, let's explore some more."

They turned left out of the Sitting Room, and descended another staircase to the saloon deck. Karen wrinkled her nose. "This is all first class again. Let's go down further, Marcus; it will be much more exciting."

"You heard what Aunt Emily said," he replied. "I think we should try to stay in her good books."

But before he could stop her, Karen had entered the elevator at the rear of the stairwell, and so he followed her reluctantly. Although as luxuriously appointed as the other areas of the ship that Marcus had seen, the elevator was sluggish, and felt as though it was riding on pulleys which were being operated manually. They stepped out onto the middle deck which bustled with people dressed noticeably differently to their wealthier counterparts who were parading their finery on the upper decks. Though most of the men wore suits, they appeared less fashionable, and flat caps were worn by a great many. The women were dressed neatly, but wore little jewellery, and none carried fans or parasols or wore large hats.

Karen, sensing Marcus's reservation about disobeying the stern aunt reclining in the ship's upper echelons, reassured him. "Don't worry, Aunt Emily won't come looking for us here." She headed off again, weaving her way around passengers until they came across an area of the deck designed for the more athletic; for there was a swimming pool, steam room, squash court, and gymnasium. They peered through the glass in the door of the gym, where a man strained at a rowing machine, dressed, it appeared, in long johns, face ruddy with exertion. There were other items of equipment in the room, one of which Marcus recognised as a type of bench-press, and behind it, a map of the world hung from the wood-panelled wall. He could pick out England, and thoughts of Christmas misted his eyes as he wished to be back home with friends and family. He tried to force himself over the reality threshold, and to will that which he knew to be real and tangible to return. But still, he was on board the enormous ship.

"What's up?" Karen asked him.

"Nothing," he replied. "I think it's time we headed back. Karen..." He faltered, searching for words. This spirit of life was not his sister, and yet he felt a bond which severed heaven and Earth, and he wanted to tell her everything and nothing.

Lunch was a formal, uncomfortable affair. Marcus was obliged to dress for the occasion in a grey flannel suit with a raised and starched collar on his shirt, and a tie which Aunt Emily tightened until he felt his eyes start to bulge with the pressure. They ate in silence in the dining saloon, and afterwards, Aunt Emily decided it was time to write letters which were to be posted from New York.

"Who are you writing to?" Marcus asked as Karen took a seat in the drawing room.

"Mother and Father, of course; and then Elizabeth and Margaret from school," she replied, opening a pad to reveal a heavily stained sheet of blotting paper. From a small case, she removed a fountain pen and a bottle of ink, which she unscrewed, pouring a small amount into an ink-well before knotting her forehead in concentration and scratching away with the pen, tutting occasionally and pausing to blot the page.

Marcus proceeded with less enthusiasm as he copied the address from Karen's letter, and the date, which was April 14th 1912. She seemed not to notice that it was almost a blank page which he placed in his envelope, signed simply:

*"Wish you were here, love Marcus."*

"Here, put mine in your envelope. It will save on postage," he offered.

"Sometimes you are strange, Marcus." She looked up from her task. "We don't need to save money on things like postage—remember the house Father has just bought?"

Marcus looked again at the name and address he

had copied from Karen. With a slow realisation, he recognised the address was that of his grandmother's parents: a mansion which had been bombed and flattened in the First World War. And the reason it was still fresh in his memory was that an envelope—and he went cold at the prospect—undoubtedly his envelope, rested on his grandmother's mantelpiece at her home in Salfords. "A memento of a dear brother lost at sea," she had once explained.

Marcus was sitting opposite his grandmother.

Alone in his cabin, Marcus sank into the deep mattress of the bed, tugging his tie free and loosening the starched collar. He brought his knees up under his chin, and looked at the four remaining stones which he had placed on the side table. No matter how long he stared, they appeared alike—though it was reasonable to conclude that the Balance was still in his possession, for the Challenge continued.

"John, Ed—can you hear me?" he called out. "Someone help me—what on Earth am I doing here?"

His plea, relayed to both the Glimmersphere and the Great Diamond Dome, was met with silence.

"Please!" He raised his voice. "I don't know what to do next."

There was a knock at the side door, and Karen entered. "Marcus, who are you talking to?" she asked.

"No-one. I was just thinking aloud," he replied.

Karen noticed the stones, and picked up one from

the table. "Where did you get these?"

"Oh, from a market somewhere, I think." Marcus tried to sound vague.

"Marcus, please may I keep this one?" she asked.

"Karen, you can't, you see..."

"Please," she pleaded. "After all, you will still have three left."

Marcus looked at her, the stone clasped to her chest so that she appeared to be praying—and he imagined his grandmother as she was now, and tried to fix her image over Karen. In his mind's eye, his grandmother faced him, grey and smiling, with hands clasped. He could visualise a chain around her neck from which there hung a small, dark object, tarnished by time. It had to be one of the stones.

"Of course you may keep it." He smiled at her, and she raced forward and brushed a kiss against his cheek.

"Thank you, I'll treasure it always." She turned to leave the cabin, calling over her shoulder, "Be ready in time for dinner, won't you?"

To Marcus, dinner that evening seemed an even more solemn occasion than lunch. Exchanges of conversation were limited in the formality of the dining saloon. Gentlemen were dressed in the immaculate uniformity of evening suits; ladies were powdered and puffed, preening in their finery, with symbols of wealth draped from porcelain necks and wrapped around fingers. The *à la carte* menu was as rich and filling as the written word suggested; and by the time the French ice cream arrived, Marcus felt as though he had eaten enough food to last a whole week.

Many of the men left for the smoking room when the meal was over. Aunt Emily ushered them back to their cabins. "Early to bed, early to rise," she said, and Marcus tumbled gratefully between the crisp, clean sheets. In his sleep, he did not notice a slight jar and rattle as the ship cut its way through the glassy, smooth ocean. The Atlantic was calm as it mirrored the stars which mingled with the lights blazing from the myriad portholes which reflected also.

In the early hours of the morning, Marcus was disturbed by Aunt Emily, who entered his cabin, her nightdress rustling as she breezed into the room.

"Marcus, come on—wake up!"

"What is it?" he asked sleepily.

"Get dressed quickly. We are to go on deck for a lifeboat drill," she explained.

Reluctantly, Marcus eased himself from the bed's warm comfort, and stumbled into his clothes. In the adjoining cabin, his aunt and sister were waiting.

"Isn't it exciting?" Karen breathed, wide-awake.

There was a light tap at the door.

"All on deck, all on deck, life jackets on." The voice was calm and authoritative.

They left the cabin, and assembled with other passengers in the foyer. Some were sleepy-eyed and questioning, some quietly bewildered, some calm and confident, others irritated at being distracted from late-night activity and entertainment. They were eased forward onto the outer deck into a bitter chill, and in the mounting confusion, a band played ragtime while crew members helped passengers into bulky life jackets.

In disbelief, they stared as a row of lifeboats was uncovered and tarpaulins were peeled away to reveal space enough for about forty people in each.

"Women and children first!" an officer cried as the crowd shuffled towards the first boat which was being prepared to be lowered. There were protests and tears as families were divided.

"But I don't want to leave you!" Marcus heard a woman sob into her husband's arms.

"You must, for the children's sake." The man tried to comfort her. "I'll take a later boat, don't worry."

Similar conversations and speculation continued.

"It's just a precaution," he heard one man explain to his wife as he helped her into the lifeboat.

"Is it really true that we've struck an iceberg?" another questioned a crew member.

"Of course it is," another passenger replied before the officer had a chance. "Look at all the ice showered on the deck below us."

The first boat was lowered over the side, swinging

gently, and illuminated by lights shining from rows of portholes. There was a faint splash when it hit the ink-black ocean and then it was away, bruising the water, and carving a path from the stationary ship.

"Don't worry, she's unsinkable..." Marcus overheard the strain of another conversation.

Another lifeboat was readied. Time swayed and was then still. The night was as cold as steel. Passengers were both calm and hysterical as a flare whooshed, heaven-bound, crackling and sprinkling artificial stars which hovered, fluttered, and then died. And the ocean below was still and peaceful.

The last boat on their side was prepared.

"Women and children only!" A man was bundled from the boat, heaved back on deck, distressed and betrayed by fear.

Aunt Emily edged them closer until they reached the front of the queue where she was taken by the hand and guided on board. Karen followed.

"I'm sorry, sir—it's women and children first." An officer blocked Marcus's path.

"But he is only a child," Aunt Emily protested. "He's only fifteen."

"I'm sorry, ma'am. There will be other boats later." The officer was polite but firm.

"Marcus!" Karen wailed, "why can't you come with us?"

"I'll catch up with you later," he said, surprised at

the calmness of his voice.

Then Karen cried out again. "Prancer—I've forgotten him! Marcus, please fetch him for me."

He remembered the unicorn which pawed the air on Karen's side-table, and the words of Moonchild: "Life is like porcelain." He could ignore neither the link nor the request, and pushed his way back through the throng towards the cabin. The foyer was clogged with passengers who were oblivious to the rising confusion and hysteria on deck, and now, as he retraced his steps along the corridor, there was a noticeable uphill effect and a resistance as he walked. The corridor was tilted at an angle. The cabin door was ajar and, as he entered, a vase slid from his aunt's bedside table and crashed to the floor. He spun around just in time to catch Prancer as he slid over the edge of Karen's table, snatching him from the air as he toppled. The unicorn was as cold as stone, and yet his eyes blazed, proud and defiant. There was both peace and power within the animal's grace and mystery. And when Marcus left the cabin, a tear rolled from Prancer's left eye, falling to the floor where it glistened like an iced miniature jewel.

He burst on to the deck, the cold clutching at his throat and stinging his eyes. The lifeboat was being lowered over the side of the tilting ship.

"Karen!" he cried, throwing Prancer into the lifeboat. Karen stood and caught the unicorn as it twisted through the air.

"Thank you, Marcus!" she shouted. In one hand, she held her porcelain unicorn—and with the other, she waved to him and blew a kiss. Then Aunt Emily pulled her back into her seat and the boat drew away from the side, swallowed slowly by the darkness which rose from the water, as cold and black as fading hope.

Another flare flew from the ship, whipped upwards to boom and sparkle—and now there was a fear which gripped people; an icy necklace choking them while they searched for more lifeboats on the starboard side of the deck. And still the band played ragtime; normality in the madness.

Marcus decided to retreat to the warmth of the deck's interior.

Here, there were even more people, crushing and pushing their way towards the outer deck; passengers from the lower reaches of the ship who had struggled to escape an advancing flood by marching through first class sections. He turned and ran back along the port side to the rear entrance, where he climbed the staircase to the next deck. Here in the smoking room, a few tables of smartly dressed men continued to play cards, triumphantly sweeping winning hands across green baize, clouded by cigar smoke. The ship's incline was more prominent on this, the top covered deck. And still they called for more drinks; one pausing to check a pocket watch which must have stopped, for he held it to his ear, tapped it, and then shrugged his shoulders, not caring at the hour while time continued to elapse and the ship tilted further.

"No, there is no hope now," he heard an officer explain to a gentleman who nodded politely. "I urge you to put this on and make a swim for it when the time comes." He held out a life jacket. The man declined the offer, and resumed his seat at the card table where he raised a glass and poured a fiery liquid down his throat before continuing the game.

Marcus approached the officer. "Is she really sinking?" he asked.

"I'm afraid so, young sir. Where are your family now?"

"My aunt and sister have left the ship on one of the lifeboats," he explained.

"Then take this. And I pray to God you may be lucky enough to find a place on another boat." The officer handed him a life jacket.

"Why do you say lucky?" Marcus asked.

"Because, sir, there are precious few lifeboats left to be launched now."

*"Marcus, you have left the stones in your cabin."* June's voice reached him.

"Thank goodness you're still with me," he breathed with relief. "Get me out of here."

"I can only help you once," June continued. "You need to collect the stones to begin with. Then we think Moonchild's words are the key."

"I remembered *'life is like porcelain'* " he said. "I had hoped that was the clue."

"It's not enough. She told you to jump where the moon swirls upon the water, and we think that is your escape route, not a lifeboat. Marcus, I have to go; the communication link is being cut. Good luck..." And then she was gone, though her words resonated still.

He cursed his foolishness at having left the stones in the cabin, then reasoned that perhaps it was meant to happen this way. The stairs were now at an angle awkward to tread, and he hugged the curvature of the wall for support. The saloon deck was strangely quiet and deserted inside. Marcus struggled along the sloping corridor towards the cabins—and when he reached B47, water lapped at his feet, rolling forward gently at first, but, by the time he had collected the three remaining stones, it had begun to advance, silent and relentless. He turned and fled to the outer deck where men jumped and yelled as they splashed into the ocean, leaping like lemmings desperate to escape.

"Abandon ship! It's every man for himself," a voice cried. "Abandon ship!"

The ocean rose to meet the deck. "Jump or you'll be

sucked down; come on, lad!" he heard someone shout.

Marcus felt enveloped by the cold, penetrating, salty sea-spray—and shouting: of madness, music, and lights, dazzling and dancing on the advancing water; echoes, the splish-splash of escape and the ship's metallic rending; the groaning and bending of its iron heart and the twisting of steel tearing below. He looked to the clear, star-sprinkled sky and there was no moon. He searched again. The ship's lights drowned while he struggled to remain on his feet, desperate to avoid the watery tomb which stretched its salty fingers; fingers which reached out to touch him and extinguish the flame of life, the last precious, precocious hope; to seep into every pore of his body and smother the last breath from within.

The ship slid further; the sea rippled darkly, and there, pale and mirrored, the moon swirled in the depths.

*"Sink or swim, but see where the moon swirls upon the water. Jump there, and you will be saved."*

He checked the sky again, star-filled, but with no moon to reflect. He looked back at the water, and there it wavered: a trembling disc, mesmerising, tantalising, and just within reach.

*"Sink or swim, sink or swim!"* This time, the madman's voice was swept in an iron wind from below—and Marcus jumped, aiming for the silver pool which

shone only for him. He entered without making a ripple, and the sea swallowed him silently as the Titanic sank also.

# 15

# Ocean Moon

At first, Marcus struggled in the silver swell, fighting the watery hands which dragged him deeper and deeper. His breath bubbled, swirling around his face, rising to break on the surface while he sank further. The frozen depths gripped him in a vice, and his lungs felt as though they would burst as he battled to resist inhaling. Just when he could bear no more and his senses started to slip away, a twinkle like a Christmas tree fairy light appeared below. Then there were several, and the water became warmer while he continued to descend. He closed his eyes and absorbed the heat. When he re-opened them, he could breathe, slowly and easily; pure, refreshing oxygen flooded his deprived lungs, and he felt no fear. His descent had slowed, and the tiny lights were all around, clustered like far-flung constellations in the distant dust of strange star systems.

Towards him swam a shape, blurred at first, and then gradually coming into focus. He recognised the form of a child with a head of golden curls, dressed in a white gown which was free flowing in the wake of the approaching swimmer.

"Marcus, at last I've found you." It was the voice of his brother.

"Aaron, what are you doing here?" he asked. The image of his brother swayed in a gentle current before him.

"I've come to take you back. Follow me, Marcus; I know a way out of this madness. We are all waiting." Aaron beckoned for him to follow.

"But how did you get here? I didn't think you were involved."

"The whole world is involved. Just drop the stones and we can go." His brother swam closer. "Just let them fall, and we can leave—come on."

Marcus examined Aaron closely, suspicious now that he had mentioned the stones. "I don't believe you," he said. "You can't be my brother, for he knew nothing of the Balance."

"It was worth a try." The pitch of the voice was raised, the expression on the face slowly changing—and while Marcus watched, the lips twisted into a cruel snarl. The teeth became hideous, dripping fangs, and the face was now scarred and twisted with evil, glaring yellow eyes. The creature's gown, tattered, ripped, and dripping with blood, fell away to reveal a goat's body, hairy and hooved, with a long, twitching, pointed tail. Two horns protruded from the creature's head and it spoke with a forked tongue.

"Give in now or be doomed! Trade me the Balance or matters will only worsen. You will never ascend, you will never ascend! Ulah Ray awaits your decision."

A cloak of darkness settled around Ulah Ray's shoulders, and his eyes burned with a glow so deep and biting that Marcus felt trapped and paralysed by fear.

"Be damned, Ulah Ray, for I shall continue." Marcus thought he had stammered with fear, but his words were remarkably clear and unwavering. "I have come this far and have good on my side."

"You fool, you will regret, you will regret!" The creature screeched with rage and brandished its talons, slashing at Marcus through the water which was now marble cold. "To continue, you must give me the password."

"But I don't know any password," Marcus protested.

"When I return, you will either know, or you will not know. The time is always the same." Ulah Ray twitched his tail, and was gone in a hiss of vapour and a trail of bubbles.

Marcus, suspended and shivering, cried out for help. "Can you hear me? I need a password, somebody...June, John, Ed, George? Can you hear me?"

"Do you wish to continue?" It was Thador who replied. "You have been through so much, and so much more awaits."

He stopped shivering. "I can go on, but tell me the password if you know it."

"Very well, Marcus. You are a worthy Keeper. When Ulah Ray returns you must say these three words: 'Neptune, help me'—and you shall be allowed to continue. In times past, Ulah Ray has deflected the words with his shield and cut them with his dagger. Now these tools are with the Light Side, thanks to you. Proceed, Marcus, proceed..." Thador's voice faded.

In a thunderous roar, the water seethed, bubbled, and receded, parting momentarily. Bearing down on him, a creature cantered, and he was rendered immobile while the skeleton of a horse reared menacingly with the figure of Ulah Ray astride its bony back, his head tilted, snarling in a wake which frothed crimson.

"The password, or failure, boy—and if you fail, I will roast your soul in Hyeelthia's deepest, most ferocious furnace. Speak now, it is time!" Ulah Ray twitched the silver reins which were threaded between his talons and the skeletal beast became still.

"Neptune, help me!" Marcus spoke the words deliberately. With a shriek of fury, Ulah Ray pulled hard on his reins and the horse reared again. Then the master and his strange steed sped like an iced whisper, accelerating so that, within a second, they were no larger than the dots of lights which hung in clusters, smaller still until there remained nothing but a thin trail of bubbles.

Marcus's breathing became increasingly difficult, short and painfully sharp. Large bubbles burst all around so that he imagined himself to be in a cauldron of boiling liquid, and there were tubes, luminescent and frothing with a green fluid. He felt completely enclosed and trapped now—and as the aeration continued and increased, throwing white foam against the tubes, ultraviolet light bathed him, and distorted voices troubled him. And all the time, breathing became more of an effort, and the light and bubbles more intense.

With a crash, Marcus broke the water's surface, and he panicked and splashed with arms flailing uncontrollably. He shouted for help. "I can't breathe, I can't breathe!"

# 16

# Delta Base 5

Suddenly, a sea of hands had hold of him, and he was pulled wriggling and dripping from the water, eyes blinking and unable to focus in the searing white light. He felt his feet on firm ground and heard a friendly voice. “It’s OK, Marcus, relax. Your detox is over for another three months.”

In the background, another voice explained. “It’s quite normal for the younger ones to experience hallucinations during the detoxification process. He’ll be fine; right now, he’s just a bit confused.”

“Where am I? I can’t see!” Marcus held out his arms, prodding the air blindly.

“Come on, calm down, Marcus. Let me help you to put these on.” He felt hands around his head and then something being strapped to his face.

“Open your eyes; you’ll be able to see now,” a woman’s voice told him calmly.

At first, he blinked painfully; then his vision returned, cloudy and swimming with colours of the spectrum bursting and rotating until the focus sharpened. He was standing, dripping, in front of a slim tank about three metres in height. It was filled almost to the top with a liquid which seemed alive as it bubbled, steamed, and changed colour as it displayed dramatic tones of green, orange, and purple. Around him stood a group of people, dressed in medical coats, surgical and sterile white, patient and smiling politely. A woman held a clipboard, upon which she made notes and ticks, pausing after each annotation to stare at him and smile, and above a door behind the group was a sign which read DETOXIFICATION UNIT.

A man stepped forward. "I'll escort you to your quarters." His voice was friendly, and he placed a hand on Marcus's shoulder and guided him in the direction of the door. "You'll probably feel like resting for a while, then you'll be functioning with one hundred per cent efficiency. There were no signs of toxin residue, so you have a clean bill of health for three months. You're in good hands; some of the prisoners in Delta Base have had such extreme cases of calcium crackle that their bones have been reduced to dust before we could treat them."

Marcus stepped shakily at the man's side into a corridor of silver and white, lined with doors and darkened windows. At one window the man paused. "DB5 Matthews, voice code open."

The window flickered into life revealing a cell in which a man sat staring blankly, head shaved, his body limp and supported by pulleys so that he resembled a bald grotesque puppet. His chest heaved slowly, and his face was pallid and beaded with perspiration.

"Request status report," Marcus's escort spoke.

"Body function maintained, status satisfactory." The reply came instantly.

"Very well, continue to monitor. Artificial organ replacement to commence as soon as Doctor Andrews is free from Detox Unit. Voice code withdrawn."

The window darkened. "What's wrong with him?" Marcus asked, troubled by the man's poor condition.

"He's just a prisoner—and as you know, when they've served their jail term in the mines, then we get to use them for our experiments. He will have the honour of being the first human to receive completely artificial body organs. Of course, he has his intact at the moment—all except his brain. That's already on its way back to Earth."

Marcus was horrified as Matthews continued. "We have made many medical advances thanks to the number of prisoners we receive, although, as I am sure your uncle—I'm sorry, the Commander—has explained, much of our research recently has been devoted to eradicating Earth's diseases. They can mutate in quite fascinating ways in our manufactured atmosphere. Airborne cancer, for example, was particularly troublesome, and meant certain death in the early days. Here we are." Matthews paused at one of the doors.

"DB5 Matthews. Prepare to receive voice code Marcus Doran."

"Online," a voice replied from a panel at the side of the door.

"Alright, Marcus, just repeat your name," Matthews instructed him.

He obliged, and the voice asked for confirmation.

"Confirmed," Matthews responded; and the door slid open to reveal Marcus's quarters.

"All the comforts of home," Matthews continued. "You won't need any special instructions. The only difference here is the viewing screen. During peak solar strength, which is 1100 to 1400 hours most days, the radiation level outside becomes lethal, and a few rads have been known to pass through unguarded viewing screens—so always close it between those hours, otherwise you'll end up in Detox before your next scheduled appointment. If you must have a view of the landscape at peak rads, switch to video, OK?" Marcus nodded.

"I'm sure the Commander will be in touch once you have rested. One other thing: the nightlife can be quite interesting outside. Sometimes we release the more troublesome inmates so that they may introduce themselves to the native nocturnals. Not a pretty sight if they're hungry, but you might enjoy the entertainment anyway. See you around." Matthews waved as he stepped back out into the corridor, and the door slid shut noiselessly behind him.

Even in his new set of unfamiliar surroundings, Marcus was weary, and although at first first his head raced with thoughts, they gradually emptied as exhaustion set in. He collapsed onto a bunk bed which appeared hard, yet seemed to absorb his body and respond to any position as he turned to get comfortable. Very soon, he was asleep and dreaming of Christmas: safely at home with family and friends, surrounded by gifts and discarded wrapping paper. There was the unique aroma of once-a-year food, pine needles, the spirit of sharing and caring, and of wellbeing and goodwill to all. And now he was back in junior school in the darkened assembly hall, dressed in white and carrying a candled Christmas Yuletide log with Mandy Whitcombe; surrounded by proud parents watching their children and singing *Once in Royal David's City.* Now the scene shifted to a snow-covered winter playground, and he was attempting to build an igloo with Anita, frozen and laughing, while a teacher's camera captured the moment as time stood still. He was suddenly at Comprehensive School on the last day of term, the classroom a cacophony of excited noise and laughter, cards delivered from the special school mailbox, torn open and cascaded on desktops. Half consciously, he thought of how precious the past seemed when you were no longer a part of it: happy, cherished moments winding away in time's tunnel, futures blaring, the action trapped yet continuing in its rightful place. The scene perpetually re-enacted by the same cast—and yet he was but a fragment of that cast, a splinter of that self which remained swimming in the pool of life where past endures. While these images of a golden childhood turned and teased, his vision began to expand like an opening book; the cover slowly eased, pages turned back, folded and gradually revealed, laying flat. A voice called to him. *"Marcus, Marcus, it's time to wake up now, it's time to wake up."*

He blinked his eyes, head clouded with sleep, and looked around for the owner of the voice. There was no-one else in the room. He swung his legs from the bunk onto the metal floor, and walked to the viewing screen.

"It's voice-activated, Marcus." He jumped, startled by the words of an invisible guest. "Do not be alarmed. I am the ultimate user-friendly computer at your service. My name is Jacqui."

He noticed a computer display positioned at a desk. "Is it you talking to me?" he asked.

"That's right, you have access to all you need to

know and more. Just ask, no reasonable request refused." The display unit flashed as each word was spoken.

"You mean you'll answer any question I ask?" Marcus began to wonder at the possibilities.

"Anything except classified information," Jacqui responded.

"OK, how about some information on this place?"

"Please specify information required."

"Location and purpose."

"Delta Base 5: penal colony and research centre specialising in genetics and synthetics. Location: Planet Crystal, Red Belt star system. First long-range, self-sufficient Delta Base, established 2575. Inmates are Category 5 prisoners: minimum term 25 years, hard labour mining ellipticinium."

"Please explain Category 5."

"Category 5 prisoners have committed crimes on Earth which carry the death sentence. They have the option to choose Delta Base 5 instead of that sentence."

"Thank you, Jacqui. Can you give me a brief outline of Earth history from 1978 to date?" Marcus asked.

"Access denied, sorry."

"Why?"

"Access denied, sorry."

The monitor fell silent, and Marcus, annoyed at having had his request refused, turned once more to the viewing screen. Remembering Jacqui's advice that it was voice activated, he spoke. "Raise viewing screen." The screen flickered into life to reveal a landscape of breathtaking colour. The ground was sprinkled with crystals which sparkled like orange snow, and stretched for as far as Marcus could see to a range of purple mountains topped by a crimson sky which faded to pink as he scaled the mountain's peaks with his vision. Despite the warm-coloured radiation glow, the scenery was hard; devoid of vegetation—or of any life, in fact—yet there were noises which could have been alien life: shrill chattering like excited monkeys, and slow, sorrowful moaning like cattle on a hot, still, summer night. While Marcus gazed in awe at the strange landscape, his door slid open quietly, and the figure of a man stepped into the room.

"So...we meet at last," he said with a sneer, and Marcus, startled, spun round to face the intruder.

"Who are you?" he asked.

"Never you mind who I am. I know who you are, and we're going for a little ride. Here, put this on. It's primitive but it will have to do." The man thrust a jump suit into Marcus's arms. "Now listen and do what I say. At the first airlock, put on your headframe. Keep your communication channel open at all times; any funny business and I've got something that will persuade you to behave." The man brandished a weapon, and Marcus recoiled instinctively.

"But where are we going?" he asked.

"I'm getting off this goddamn planet," the man replied, stepping into his own space suit. "As for you... well, I'm not sure where you're going. Now, let's move it."

They stepped into the metallic corridor and stopped at the first airlock.

"Right, it's voice activated." The man spoke in hushed tones. "Repeat these words: 'DB5 Doran, activate airlock'. The computer will ask for confirmation, and you just say 'confirmed', OK?"

Marcus nodded and repeated the instruction. The first door of the airlock lifted, and they moved forward into the inner chamber. The man lifted a helmet onto his head which snapped quickly into place, and the darkened visor hid his features completely so that he could have been anyone. He adjusted a series of dials on his suit and, seeming satisfied, turned his attention to Marcus. He checked a row of similar controls, and then twisted Marcus's head to check the security of the head-frame.

"OK, now can you hear me?" the man asked. His voice was loud and clear in the head-frame.

"Sure," Marcus replied.

"Right, let's move it—you're my passport to freedom."

The outer door of the airlock lifted, and they

stepped onto the surface of the planet Crystal. The gleaming, baked orange dust crunched underfoot. Directly in front was a vehicle equipped for rough terrain, not unlike a bulldozer for it had caterpillar tracks. The man propelled Marcus on board and into a cabin which resembled an aircraft cockpit containing an array of instruments. The equivalent of a car's windscreen, tinted and toughened, provided the only view. The man pressed a button which sealed the cabin, and another which fired the vehicle's engine into life. Two safety harnesses dropped from the roof and clicked automatically around them.

"Do I have to keep my helmet on? It's really uncomfortable," Marcus complained.

"Yes; we're going beyond the reach of atmospheric control, so unless you want to spend an intensive session in Detox, I suggest you keep it on." The man coaxed the vehicle forward and it gained speed gradually, shuddering and wavering slightly as the tracks gripped and crunched their way across the planet's crust. Like a pilot, the man monitored the vehicle's instruments, checking and re-checking LED displays while he maintained a course towards the purple mountains. A whining sound filled the cabin, and when it had faded, the man explained: "Atmosphere warning. We're on our own. Your body weight is now one quarter of what you're accustomed to."

While they continued, the man attempted radio

contact. "DB5 Jordan hailing Red Belt. Request safe passage; have valuable hostage—repeat, have valuable hostage."

Now that his status had been confirmed, Marcus shrank into the harness as doom and despair enveloped him. Jordan was obviously a Delta Base inmate, and his imagination ran riot in speculation of the crimes the man may have committed. At the very least he was a murderer, and at most...Marcus tried to think of something else.

The radio in the cabin crackled into life. *"DB5 to Miner 611. Please identify user code; you are entering a restricted area. Above average rads—repeat, above average rads."*

Jordan slammed the instrument panel with his fist and closed the channel.

"Damn you," he whispered. "There *must* be a pirate ship out there somewhere."

He switched frequency and repeated his previous message which was met only with the crackle of space static. And now, as the vehicle advanced, Marcus detected a faint rise in temperature: a noticeable increase which was not yet uncomfortable. Jordan became increasingly irritated at the lack of response to his radio request, and then began to concentrate his attention on a group of instruments in the cabin which flashed at increasingly regular intervals and seemed to be causing him concern.

"What's up?" Marcus asked, his fear of speaking to Jordan now overcome by the fear of uncertainty.

The flash of the instrument panel reflected in Jordan's head-frame, and gave him the appearance of an alien while he cursed and coaxed the vehicle closer to the mountains which loomed ever closer, their purple peaks soaring to the crimson sky which dripped like blood onto the landscape.

"Increasing rads and decreasing fuel," Jordan replied, "and at this intensity, the solar panels will have burnt out."

He resumed his concentration, and now the heat began to irritate; prickly heat like a combination of wool against bare, sunburnt skin, and of grass against a back fresh from a swimming pool. Marcus wriggled in discomfort, pinned to his seat by the harness. As the temperature rose, so the speed of the vehicle decreased, and the tone of the engine changed.

"Damn!" Jordan exclaimed, once again slamming the instrument panel with his gloved fist. "We'll have to travel the rest of the way on foot."

He flicked a series of switches which seemed to inject the engine with a temporary boost of power. When it had been absorbed and used, the motor cut out and they coasted while the radio crackled and the caterpillar tracks carved their path through the crystalline orange snow. The vehicle shook to a halt, a useless shell in an empty world. Jordan released the harnesses and lifted a box from the floor of the cabin from which he extracted a number of containers. He clipped several of them around his waist and onto various panels on his suit, then repeated the procedure on Marcus.

"Before we disembark, a quick run through." Jordan pointed at the first container clipped to his waist. "Anti-rad boost." He moved to each in turn. "Oxygen, food, water, body toxin removal unit, temperature control. Your main concern is with the first unit; it's set at maximum and must stay at that level until we reach the mountains. Your second concern is temperature control, also set at maximum. We've got about an hour before we'll be either fried alive or roasted by radiation, so let's move it."

Jordan ripped the communicator from the control panel and released the cabin door lock.

"Isn't it safer to stay here?" Marcus asked.

"Not a chance. We're directly under the Red Belt. Just before night shift every rotation, this whole area —the crystal orchard—is bombarded with the radioactive crystals you can see on the ground. They slice through anything known to man, so we might just as well head for the caves." Jordan stepped from the cabin and glided to the glittering ground. Marcus followed, and they bounded and bobbed their way forward, half running, half leaping in the lower gravity level. For Marcus, the novelty of reduced-weight walking and the concentration required to hold the line that Jordan was taking were a distraction from the severity of the situation. After twenty minutes of exertion, Jordan stopped and looked back, allowing Marcus to catch up. A cloud of dust hovered where they had trodden, leaving footprints which gaped in the orange crust.

"Our trail will be covered by the Red Belt storm," Jordan said while he checked the anti-rad boost and temperature control units on their suits and, seeming satisfied, continued towards the foot of the mountains.

Marcus found it increasingly difficult to match Jordan's pace, soon falling behind, and, in frustration, slipping so that he fell sideways, grazing against the ground so that the crystals slashed into his suit, ripping at the material so that it hung in shreds from his side. There was a hiss of escaping oxygen and coolant which splashed onto the planet's surface where it bubbled and evaporated, a wisp of vapour carried away by a silent wind. Immediately the temperature within Marcus's suit rose alarmingly and he shouted out to Jordan. "Help, my suit's ripped, I'm burning up!"

Jordan responded. "Hold on, I'll be right with you." The fugitive landed at his side and helped him to his feet while inspecting the damage to the suit. He flipped open a panel in his own suit to reveal a repair kit from which he took an assortment of tools. Deftly cutting and clipping like a surgeon, Jordan rejoined Marcus's air and coolant hoses before turning his attention to the suit's ripped fabric which he melted together with a fine jet of spray.

"You've lost some oxygen and coolant," Jordan reported.

"How much is left?" Marcus asked, worried at the diagnosis.

Jordan laughed. "Enough; we'll be either radiated, eaten by wildlife, or caught by DB5 Patrol before you run out. Now come on, we don't have much time. Peak rads coincides with maximum sun-stab; then it's storm time—and I'd rather be watching that than be in it."

They were completely in the shadow of the mountains now, protected from the worst of the glare, and Marcus could see the cave entrances towards which they were heading. He could also see the first signs of native life; heat-twisted shrubs bearing purple berries, giving the appearance of gnarled, grotesque Christmas trees.

"I thought nothing survived the storms," he remarked.

"Nothing does," Jordan replied. "Those bushes have a life cycle of one rotation."

As Marcus brushed by one of the shrubs, there was

a screech; and a creature which looked like a red armadillo, disturbed from feeding on the berries, scampered away in the direction of the caves.

"What was that?" Marcus asked.

"Nothing to worry about," Jordan said calmly, "just a small herbivore. It's the rest of the food chain above it that we have to be wary of."

Marcus gulped, recalling Matthews's comments about the native nocturnals. "What are they like?" he stammered, unable to control his fear or to conceal his vulnerability.

"The official description is 'particularly voracious carnivores'. I've come close to a few down the mines during night shift. Some would call me lucky; they picked off the other miners in the gang I was in. Some would call me unlucky, because I've lived long enough to be used for DB5 experiments."

They arrived at a row of gaping black cave entrances, and at each there lay a pile of bones which had been picked completely dry. While they stood, a group of spindly-legged creatures with heads like that of an octopus each selected a pile and began to crunch at the bones as if they were sweets, snapping and chewing, undisturbed by Marcus and Jordan, the uninvited witnesses of the strange feast.

"We must find a cave without bones at the entrance," Jordan commanded, and motioned to Marcus to follow to his right. A few minutes more and there were several entrances which appeared bone-free. Jordan reached into his tool kit and pointed a device like a Geiger counter into one of the caves.

"What's that?" Marcus asked.

"It's a heat and movement detector. No sign of either in there, so hopefully it's carnivore-free. Come on," he said, and he led the way into the cave. Because of the insulation provided by the spacesuit and head-frame, Marcus could detect no change in atmosphere or temperature as they entered the foot of the purple mountains. But he imagined being swallowed by the cavernous blackness, surrounded by the bleak drip of ebony walls and slowly shuffling footsteps on the sandy floor, as the invisible demons of darkness prepared to pounce, devour, and then toss his bones carelessly to be chewed by the creatures feeding outside.

Jordan halted when the Red Belt radiation from outside began to pale. He lowered the communicator to the ground, and snapped two small boxes from its side which he turned in his gloved hands. He reached into his toolkit once more for what appeared to be nothing more than a screwdriver, and within seconds, there was a high-pitched tone as the boxes came to life, with two red lights flashing alternately on top of each. Jordan placed them carefully on the ground some three metres apart, and a laser beam cut upwards, bouncing from the roof of the cave and carving a perfect circle around them, passing through each box.

Jordan explained. "It's an artificial atmosphere which will protect us from radiation and provide us with oxygen. It's also an energy shield to guard against unwelcome visitors." He removed his head-frame. "...Or occupants," he added, as he scanned the cave's interior.

Marcus did likewise, relieved to be free from the restrictions of the head-frame. The air provided by the unit was fresh, and the temperature comfortable. Jordan kneeled over the communicator and resumed his attempts to contact a passing pirate ship. Despite the fact that he was essentially a hostage, Marcus felt more at ease with Jordan—and although he had been abrupt and desperate when he had burst into his quarters, he did not seem to be a volatile maniac. What were probably once finely chiselled features were now sad and hollow, emaciated almost, with signs of suffering and endurance on a battle-scarred face. But his eyes burned brightly, like defiant flashing daggers in the dark while he toiled with the communicator.

"If I am the Commander's nephew, why don't you bargain for your freedom with him?" Marcus asked quietly.

"What do you mean, *if* you are?" Jordan snapped back.

"I mean, of course I am. I just wondered why you didn't try to strike a deal back at Delta Base," Marcus added hastily.

Jordan relaxed his efforts and leaned back against the communicator. "Everywhere has its place. This isn't what I'd call home. I wanted to go back to Earth, or at least to a planet close to Earth. The trouble with Delta Base is that the only ships to visit are the shuttles which bring fresh prisoners and take away ellipticinium—and any interesting experiments that the barbarians who masquerade as doctors perform. Of course, there have been attempts to escape before; twice with hostages, which resulted in the prisoners gaining safe passage from Delta Base—but, you see, on a ship which is known, it is easy to hyper-bounce the prisoner back to this awful planet. I would rather take my chances with an unknown pirate ship with you as insurance against attack, and demand that a ransom be paid to the captain and crew for your safe return. My motive is purely freedom, not financial reward."

"What crime did you commit back on Earth?" Marcus asked.

"I carried the blame for a political assassination. I suppose I hold my beliefs in a fanatical kind of way," Jordan half laughed as he replied.

"You mean you're not really a murderer?" Marcus was surprised.

"No, not me." Jordan looked out to the crystal landscape which burned intensely as he shielded his eyes with a hand. "At least we missed peak rads."

The communicator suddenly burst into life. *"This is Captain Reynolds of Angel Halo calling DB5 Jordan. Request proof of cargo—repeat, request proof of cargo. I have Marcus Doran's voice code computer linked, ready to run."*

Jordan signalled Marcus towards the communicator. "Just say who you are and who you are with."

Marcus knelt and spoke. "This is Marcus Doran and I am with Jordan from Delta Base 5."

There was a delay of a few seconds while the message sped through space to the approaching vessel.

*"Confirmed. Undertaking safety scan. Estimated arrival time within one hour following Red Belt storm. Please keep frequency open in meantime."*

"Message received and understood," Jordan responded, and boosted the signal strength of the communicator.

The outside glare was quickly gone like a candle being snuffed out, the remaining light fading and wraithlike. From the darkness which followed came a rumble; and then, with a raging roar, the sky erupted. Flashing torrents of icy orange rained death onto the planet, with the wind sweeping up the mantle of the crystal orchard and dashing it like desert dust. They could hear the howling of the ferocious wind and the crashing of unseen clouds, but could not feel the storm as they watched from the safety of the energy shield within the cave. The invisible wall which protected them sparked at each stray sliver which sliced at them, cutting at the energy field like a small scythe before being deflected to the floor, or to whirl like a miniature cracker-jack against the cave walls. In the violence of the storm, the whole planet seemed to lift and breathe in deeply, drinking the turbulence until it subsided, gone as quickly as it had come, leaving the landscape exactly as before once the veil of dust had settled. It was then that Marcus noticed a hollow moan blowing from the back of the cave, and a scratching sound like metal on ice; the thump of a great footstep, and a hiss like steam escaping under pressure. They both turned round at the same time to face a row of red eyes glowering at them. There was a menacing shuffle, a scrape, and another thud on the floor as something slithered closer, while all around the sound of heavy breathing and the stench of rotting flesh filled the air.

The sound of movement subsided momentarily, but the creature's breathing hissed like ice through the cave as its eyes burned hungrily.

"What is it?" Marcus dared to whisper.

"It sounds like one of the larger carnivores," Jordan replied, "which could be bad news, because it's just about dinner time and I think it thinks we are on the menu."

As Jordan finished his sentence, something whirled through the air, sparking against the shield, and clattering to the cave floor where it lay white and broken: a huge bone glistening with saliva. Then there was a roar like the storm's anger. In a rush of momentum from the darkness came a creature monstrous and grotesque; a huge beast with five eyes ablaze with red fury, hairy and tusked like a mammoth, teeth flashing, snapping, and flesh threatening. They recoiled in terror as it launched itself at them only to slap and thud like dark thunder against an invisible wall. With increased rage, the carnivore raised itself on its haunches to a height of about three metres, and lunged forward, displaying three pairs of powerful limbs armed with razor-sharp talons ready to slash. The shield showered the beast with sparks as it pressed hungrily against the barrier, and its matted fur became foul-smelling flames which spread quickly from its belly, sending it into convulsions of pain and fury. It charged once more, and this time the shield was unable to deflect the full force. The momentum of the assault was absorbed, but the creature seemed to come in closer, as though the wall was being stretched. For a split second, it was nearly upon them, and they could feel its breath and see its cruel teeth, stained and dripping. Then it dropped away and ran from the cave, bellowing in pain, its fur burning like straw.

Jordan sighed with relief, and dropped to his knees to examine the life support unit. Then he cursed quietly.

"What's wrong?" Marcus asked.

"That creature has compromised the unit's efficiency. If we're attacked again, the shield may not deflect one hundred per cent, and I can't recharge the solar packs until sun-stab."

Marcus looked to the cave's entrance at the planet's tinted distance. "It still looks light outside."

"That's radiation glow," Jordan explained. "Sun-stab isn't for another two hours or so."

The communicator crackled into life again. *"This is Captain Reynolds of Angel Halo calling DB5 Jordan. Request landing code. Repeat, request landing code."*

Jordan knelt at the communicator and opened the response channel. "This is DB5 Jordan. Programme landing code DB5 0X."

Captain Reynolds replied almost immediately. *"Access denied. Request alternative."*

Jordan turned away from the communicator. "Damn them!" He hit the cave floor in frustration. "They've changed the landing code."

He re-opened the response channel. "Suggest hyper-bounce. We are at grid reference Q18 T4."

*"We have you fixed, Jordan,"* Reynolds replied, *"but there's a hyper-bounce blanket in operation."*

"Surely there's a gap somewhere?"

*"Our scan revealed none. We have time for two orbits only. If status changes, I will communicate further. Please keep your frequency open."*

Jordan was silent, and kneeled as though praying at the communicator. All at once, he was sad and lonely; a figure of despair, trapped by the mapped fate of the stars. An insignificant life in an endless universe; a life ebbing as an ocean recedes, its time ticking away and stolen by relentless seconds. He shook uncontrollably as tears splashed down his face, dripping onto the dust at his knees, where his grief collected in pools to be absorbed slowly.

Marcus felt his sadness and spoke softly. "Maybe we should try to get some sleep."

There was still no reply, so he curled up in the sand while Jordan still sat with head bowed, gently rocking, the shape of a halo bathed around him from the soft shadows and the radiation.

In the silvery trinket half-gloom, Marcus half slept, half dreamed as George's voice seeped into his mind with an osmosis that took a while to sharpen and focus. And he could see his friend's face as a reflection on a pool, rippling when he spoke so that his image became water-blurred.

*"Marcus, we can see the last part of the Hyeelthia poem written on the cave wall. It must be your next clue. You are in the crystal orchard; wait for the signal and guard the Balance. Of the three stones that remain, you must choose*

*one, and we cannot tell which is true."*

George's face disappeared completely, washed away by the water to be replaced by the last six lines of the Hyeelthia poem daubed onto one of the walls within the cave, and accompanied by Neanderthal illustrations flickering in the eerie illumination of a torch of rushes. They depicted strange beasts, monsters similar to that which had attacked them earlier—devilish bats huddled and hanging from a cave roof, and the most evil and chilling image: that of Ulah Ray astride his skeletal steed, a horn raised to his lips; the master of darkness at the head of the hunt. And in the trance of torch-flame light, his eyes glared from the wall, three dimensional and shifting.

When sun-stab pierced the crystal dawn, Marcus was awake, lying in the sand, mesmerised by the planet's cold beauty; the sky dripping with the colours of the rainbow while he watched the light stretch from night-time into day. He reached inside his jump suit for the remaining stones which clinked like marbles in his palm. "At least they're still safe," he thought, relieved that they had survived the journey into the unknown.

He turned to look for Jordan, who was awake also, and preparing to recharge the shield which was lowered momentarily while he ran a line from one of the energy boxes to the solar panel, which was then placed outside the cave.

"What are you going to do now?" Marcus asked.

"Sit tight for a bit longer," Jordan replied. "DB5 Patrol will be almost upon us by now, but so is another Red Belt storm, judging by the static on the communicator."

Marcus was puzzled. "I thought the storm came only before nightfall?"

"It does as a rule, but it has been known for two to occur in one rotation." The ground began to thump and rumble. "I think we've got company again," he added.

Jordan raised the energy shield's level to maximum, and the huge carnivore came into view, lumbering towards the cave—and as it drew near, they could see evidence of its night-time harvest: other creatures of dusk gathered up in its limbs; carcasses hanging limp and ragged. Marcus and Jordan retreated so that their backs were against the wall, and the beast halted at the entrance where it slurped greedily, tearing and chewing ravenously at the raw meat, and throwing bones idly to the ground. When it had eaten its fill, it stood and belched noisily before gathering the remainder of its feast and dragging it past them, and into the rear of the cave.

"It's left something behind." Marcus pointed to the floor where a yellow object lay throwing a shaft of light to the roof.

Jordan turned away.

“What’s wrong?” Marcus asked.

“It’s a miner’s hat. That monster has been down the mines.”

Before Marcus could share in Jordan’s revulsion, the cave was filled with a new sound, one which evoked an immediate reaction from the fugitive. He pushed Marcus to the floor and scrambled towards the boxes which maintained the shield, pulling in the solar panel and closing the hailing channel on the communicator.

“Don’t say a word,” Jordan ordered. “It’s a seeker.”

The sound varied in pitch, exploring the cave and bouncing its findings back to DB5 Patrol, who were now within striking range of the mountains.

Marcus lay flat on the floor, his face pressed against the sand until Jordan gave the all-clear.

“Time to move out—quickly,” he urged, “I’m turning off the shield, so put your head-frame on. Now!”

He gathered up the instruments while Marcus struggled to replace his head-frame and re-engage the life support systems of his suit. After a swift check, Jordan led the way out of the cave, only to stop in his tracks, a yell of despair ringing in Marcus’s ears via the head-frame communication channel.

“Stay back,” he shouted. “I’m caught in a locator!”

Jordan, immobilised by the Patrol, screamed as the full fury of another Red Belt storm sliced though his suit, the deadly slivers reducing his bones to dust within seconds. And as Marcus stared in disbelief, all that remained—his very last image of Jordan—was that of an orange aura around his head frame which glimmered and then shattered to be blown towards the horizon.

Marcus froze, numbed by Jordan's disappearance into the wind. He continued to stare at where the man had stood, expecting him to materialise. A stray sliver of orange crystal rebounded inside the cave, slicing through Marcus's suit, and gashing him just below his left knee. He drew in a sharp breath at the waves of stinging pain that followed, and hastily retreated, forced further towards the rear of the cave as the storm intensified and more crystals found their way inside, bouncing and rebounding, closer and closer, until he reached a bend where they no longer seemed able to penetrate—and which threw him into complete darkness, so that not even the light of the storm could be seen.

Marcus leaned back against the cave wall, feeling for the stones once more which nestled in his gloved hand, glowing slightly like infrared eggs. Suddenly, the wall gave—just a fraction, but enough to cause him to over-compensate by leaning forward to maintain his balance—and he stumbled. Then the wall moaned and heaved. A great, dark, dank, breathing mass. Five red eyes burning again with hell's fire, a slash of talons, and the click of dagger teeth. Marcus leapt around the bend, the creature behind him, the Red Belt storm in front, a dazzle of orange snow and radiation. He was trapped, searching desperately for an exit, left or right—but there was none; and from behind, he could hear the slither and bellow of the cave-dwelling carnivore, disturbed from its slumber and hungry again. As he stood on the brink, the precipice of dilemma, the hunted forced into a corner, trapped on the edge of eternity, a sound vibrated through his whole body. A sound that he could feel; a far-away horn which beckoned him, teasing his senses, capturing his fear; and alluring, like soft daybreak. And it signalled to him from the centre of the storm.

He moved towards the entrance, clasping the stones' cold comfort. At his first step, a huge taloned limb crashed to the floor where he had stood, finding nothing but his footprints. He stopped at the point where he had witnessed Jordan's destruction at oblivion's dividing line. And the horn blew again, low and mournful, sweet sorrow from the storm's hard heart. Marcus stepped forward, an orange aura in a syrup sunset over the crystal orchard where he was swallowed by the tempest, sliced and brushed by dust so that only a lonely note remained, until that too was carried away in the wild wind.

# 17

# The Court of Ulah Ray

In the court of Ulah Ray, Marcus stood in the dock, flanked by two enormous bats. There was no jury, but below him, images of the Glimmersphere and Chamber hovered above a mist which covered the floor of the courtroom. Facing him was Ulah Ray, red-gowned and peering at him severely from beneath a silver-grey wig. He raised a great hammer, and brought it crashing down onto a wooden block. The crack of wood upon wood echoed in shock waves around the room, causing Marcus to jump.

"How does the prisoner plead? Guilty, or not guilty?" Ulah Ray shrieked, and the two bats at Marcus's side twitched in anticipation.

The voice of Thador was relayed calmly from the image of the Glimmersphere. "Admit to nothing, Marcus, or he will imprison your soul."

"Silence in court," the strange judge snapped. "How does the prisoner plead?" he repeated.

"What's the charge?" Marcus asked.

Ulah Ray again slammed the hammer onto the block. "You answered my call, did you not? Surely that makes you guilty, boy?"

"I have committed no crime," Marcus said quietly but firmly. "If this is the end of the Challenge, I would like to return to Christmas."

At the mention of Christmas, Ulah Ray's faced turned purple—and thunder and storm-clouds crashed in his eyes as he leaned forward, wagging a bony finger.

"There will be no mention of that here," he hissed.

"Do you mean the Challenge or Christmas?" Marcus asked.

"Enough!" Ulah Ray screamed. "Send for the other prisoners."

From the image of the Chamber in the Great Diamond Dome, the Master of Thoughts spoke. "Ulah Ray, it was agreed that only the Temporary Keeper should be involved directly in the Challenge. There can be no other prisoners."

"Ha! The other little humans—they all have a link with the Balance; therefore, they are involved, and I demand that they be sent to me. After all, it is the final stage of the Challenge. Send for the other prisoners," he repeated.

Thador spoke again. "The Master of Thoughts is right. We all agreed that the Temporary Keeper alone should receive the Challenge."

"I am the judge here," Ulah Ray roared, "and I demand that they all participate in the final stage. After all, the more of them there are, the greater the chance of them succeeding."

"Ulah Ray, you lie," the Master of Thoughts bellowed. "If they each have to succeed, then the odds are very much stacked in your favour."

"What is the last stage?" Marcus asked. "Am I allowed to know?"

"You will wait until sentence is passed!" Ulah Ray cried. "This trial is adjourned."

The courtroom grew dark, and Marcus was led away by his guards to a cell into which he was shoved roughly. The door was slammed ominously shut, the key twisted in the great lock, and the enormous bats shuffled away with a scratch of claws and leather on the stone floor.

In the darkened courtroom, a heated conversation raged between Ulah Ray and the images of The Master of Thoughts, Carnyx, and Thador.

"Both sides of the Chamber acknowledge that this is the Dark Side's strongest challenge for centuries," said The Master of Thoughts, "but it is only by chance that such an opportunity has arisen."

"Nonsense!" Carnyx spoke from the Glimmersphere. "It has arisen as a result of human frailty and greed. On Adam's head be it, for he was trusted by the Light Side and failed them."

"Adam failed no-one but himself!" Thador retorted. "And you are a fine one to talk about greed. See how quickly you came back through time to claim the Balance. It belongs in its rightful place beneath the Image."

"It belongs opposite the Image." Ulah Ray spat out the last word. "I have had many disguises throughout history, and each time the Balance has been held by the Dark Side, I have returned more cunning and invigorated. I grow tired of my better known image. The chains of time are stretching; a new era awaits."

"Enough of your fanaticism, Dark One," The Master of Thoughts interrupted. "The final stage of the Challenge awaits."

Marcus paced his prison cell anxiously. He had searched for a way out, but there was no other door and no window. There was no natural light, and if there had been an escape route he could not be sure it would have led him to safety—or anywhere for that matter.

A table and chair of stone were the cell's only cold furniture, and from the centre of the table, there burned a crimson flame fed by an invisible fuel. Steady, unwavering, giving the room an otherworldly atmosphere and secrecy, and a damp warmth filled with trickery and seclusion.

"Call the prisoner!" a voice cried, and the scratching footsteps returned along the corridor. Marcus felt an adrenaline surge, the instinct to flee from his tormentors, as the key to his cell was again turned in the lock. The bats led him away to the courtroom, and back into the wooden box of the dock. There was an additional presence: a frog-like creature sitting in front of the dais writing notes, so that Marcus guessed it to bc thc clerk of the court.

"All stand!" the creature cried as Ulah Ray swept into the room, ermine-and-velvet-gowned, with his wig flowing into his robes.

There was still no jury, and Marcus and his guards were already standing. When Ulah Ray was seated, the images of the Glimmersphere and Chamber reappeared from the misty floor.

"Clerk of the court, please hand me the jury's verdict." Ulah Ray leaned forward and snatched a piece of paper from the frog.

"Let the defendant step forward!" Marcus was pushed roughly to the front of the dock.

Ulah Ray continued: "Marcus Doran, you have been found guilty of progressing to the final stage of the Challenge, set to decide the Balance of Power on Future Earth. In accordance with the law of Hyeelthia, you will be taken from here to the Nightmare Maze, where you will be joined by your friends from Earth Past. To succeed in the final stage, you are all required to escape from the maze, and from the nightmares that you yourself have created through time. If you escape from the maze you will have the home advantage in a final, fateful game of Forty-Forty where the base will be known as Owl House, and which only you need reach in order to ascend your mind's throne. If, at any time, you wish to halt the final stage, simply surrender the Balance and all will be well. Clerk of the court, you may record the verdict. Take the prisoner away..."

Ulah Ray's voice faded as a wind swept through the courtroom, fluttering papers which swirled like white leaves down into the mist. A roar like water rushing through a canyon filled the air, causing Marcus to clamp his hands over his ears. The wind pushed hard and hurt his eyes so that he was forced to close them; so strong that it stole his breath away. Then the room shook, and he began to spin, cartwheeling through space; everything changing, yet nothing occurring. Opaque horizons sliding, the beginning and the end of time shaking and spiralling, kaleidoscope patterns eternal and free. Then, with a bump, he landed on solid ground, and slowly opened his eyes.

# 18

# The Nightmare Maze

"Marcus, Marcus, you're here! Thank goodness you're safe." It was June; and, as his vision cleared like a picture book slowly opening, she was running towards him on lush grass walled by high privet hedges strung with cobwebs which glistened; sliding through shiny morning dew until she reached his side, breathless and dreamy in the early morning light.

Before he could even greet her, she continued: "We watched and felt everything. You've done so well, but now we have to escape from the maze. Thador argued your case well, and if we can find a way out quickly, your nightmares may not reach us."

"It's great to see you, June." Marcus hugged her, then stepped back to survey their surroundings. "It looks like the maze at Hampton Court, or the one at Blackgang Chine on the Isle of Wight...but where are George, Ed, and John?"

"I don't know," June replied. "I've called out for

them, but they must be in a different part of the maze."

"How long have you been here?" he asked.

"It seems like about ten minutes, but I can't be sure. Thador says the Glimmersphere has locked us in time, so that although it feels like the Challenge has lasted for days, it's still Christmas Eve, really. Which way shall we try?"

"We might as well keep going in this direction. John, Ed, can you hear me?" he yelled. There wasn't a murmur on the still air. The soft summer daybreak sun stretched at their feet, and soon the dew began to rise in sweet, warm wisps. The turns in the maze were right-angled, and the path Marcus chose led them dizzily to a dead end, and to a thick wall of high privet which enclosed them. There was a plaque on the ground at the foot of the hedge, stained and aged by the elements, and June stooped curiously to read it, brushing its surface with her hand, and blowing dust from the etched lettering.

*"Linger no longer than now,"* she read the inscription. "What does it mean, I wonder?"

"I don't know, but I think we should try to look over the hedge. June, try standing on my shoulders and see if you can find a way out."

Marcus crouched as June climbed onto his shoulders. He gripped her forearms and rose slowly, shaking slightly and leaning into the hedge for support.

"Can you see anything?" his voice was muffled by the hedge.

"I can't quite see over. I'll try to pull myself right up." June pushed away from him and hauled herself to the top.

Marcus tried to step back but found that he could not. Embedded in the hedge face first, he was immobilised by a series of strong twig-like hands which tightened their grip as the hedge rustled and crackled. He struggled, unable to open his eyes because of the foliage smothering his face, and felt trapped and claustrophobic as he fought for breath.

Then Thador's voice spoke, clear and soothing like a bell chiming over water. *"Understand your dreams, Marcus, understand your dreams."*

He ceased struggling and wondered at the words. "Help me! What do you mean?" He mouthed the sentence but it was suffocated by the privet.

Thador replied. *"This is your nightmare, Marcus. What you have created, you may overcome."*

He was calmer now, trying to reason; logic versus dream. This was a re-enactment of a past nightmare. One in which he had been swallowed, smothered, and suffocated by bony, invisible hands which had pushed him deeper into the terror abyss from which there was no escape. He had woken crying in the night, perspiring and delirious from influenza and horror dreams. To break free from that nightmare, he had woken up; yet this was very real, and he was very much awake. June, triumphant at reaching the top of the hedge found nothing but a mantle of darkness which completely cloaked any view that the advantage of height may have afforded; though when she looked down to where Marcus stood embedded in the privet, it was daylight.

"Marcus, it's completely dark up here—I can't see a thing!" she cried. When there was no response, she peered down from her leafy platform. "Marcus, why don't you step back now?" Then she could see the reason why he did not, as rows of twitching twig-shaped foliage fingers snatched at him and wove him into the wall.

Suddenly, they were upon her too, rising in a shuffle of leaves and a wooden crackle to grab her and drag her down. Like Marcus she fought and writhed, but sank, kicking and yelling, and the more she contorted and wriggled, the greater her rate of descent—until the hedge shook no longer, and she was swallowed completely; a prisoner within the wall of the maze and the paralysis created by Marcus's dream delirium.

Below her, Marcus searched his mind for a method of escape. *"What you have created, you may overcome."* The words replayed in his head with torment in their simplicity. Now that he had stopped struggling—without realising it initially—movement within the wall had become possible as he stretched slowly, seeking a more comfortable position. There was less tension, more space, and the snatching fingers seemed to have lessened their grip.

He stood and swept a gradual arc with his hands, carving a semi-circle above his head. There was no resistance; all was quiet.

"June," he called, "can you hear me?"

"Marcus!" She sounded quite close. "I'm trapped up here. I can't move."

"Try to relax," he told her, "then make an arc above your head with your hands."

There was a moment's silence before she spoke again. "It worked. I can move. I pushed out slowly with my hands, like doing the breaststroke in swimming—and I'm sure I moved upwards."

Marcus did the same, kicking gently with his feet until he was level with her. "You're right, it works," he greeted her. "Use your feet as well; let's see if we can swim our way out."

They pushed away together, slipping through the dull void, rising to break the surface where the privet parted and the sun dazzled their eyes. But before they could look out over the expanse of the maze, the hedge tilted, and sent them tumbling to the ground where their fall was cushioned by clumps of grass.

*"Linger no longer than now!"* Ulah Ray's reedy voice,

cynical and caustic, cascaded around them—and, needing no second warning, they picked themselves up and ran without looking back.

When Marcus paused to catch his breath, drawing in great lungfuls of fresh air, June looked at him. "If that's just the start of your nightmare creations, I don't feel like meeting the rest. What other surprises have you invented?"

"There must be hundreds to choose from," he gasped. "I'm sorry about that one, but there are worse to come if we don't find the others and discover a way out."

"Perhaps they have already escaped."

He shrugged a "maybe" and started walking, taking care to avoid the sides of the hedges, and steering a clear course down the middle of the path. But after a couple of minutes, they still had not come across another turning. The maze was like a long, green corridor which appeared to stretch for miles in either direction.

"This can't be right," said June, as they continued. "We're never going to find our way out along here."

They stopped, and as they did so, the walls on either side continued.

"They're moving forwards," Marcus pointed out.

"Either that, or we're going backwards," June agreed. "Try walking on."

The walls appeared to stop, but they made no progress as they walked, for the ground was moving backwards, and their pace merely maintained their status within the maze, even when it quickened, for the ground compensated immediately.

"This is hopeless. We might just as well take a rest and wait for a gap to appear." Marcus sat, exhausted, on thc ground, and June joined him.

"If this is just a conveyor belt taking us back to the start, we'll never get out," she complained.

"It might even take us to the exit," Marcus said hopefully. While they sat, a gap appeared, and passed before they could move.

"We might as well be ready for the next one—if there is a next one." June rose to her feet, and examined the hedge wall as it passed, searching for an alternative path within the maze.

"Quickly, Marcus—here comes one now."

He stood at her side as a new path revealed itself, and they stepped into it, grateful for a break in the monotony, grateful for the chance of another exit. The path widened gradually, and as it did, the walls on either side became lower and lower, trimmed to head height, then waist, then ankle level. Then they were gone, and the pathway opened into a large, ghostly, Victorian English garden with massive mowed lawns; lush and undulating, bordered with magnificent flower beds; weeping willows, dreamy and bowed. In the middle of the lawns stood a breathtaking statue, centre stage and proud, pawing the air, carved from the purest white marble so that it shone like an angel.

"It's Prancer!" Marcus exclaimed as he ran towards the Unicorn. They stood in awe at the statue's splend-our and pristine purity. Prancer's name shone from a golden plate at the base of the monument.

"What's he doing here?" June wondered.

"Perhaps he's from my dreams as well—but surely he is good; a symbol of the Light Side." Marcus circled the Unicorn. "It's good to see you again, boy," he said, as they turned to continue through the garden, not noticing the tear which glistened in Prancer's right eye before rolling down his face and onto the lawn where it shone amongst the clover.

"I'm beginning to feel hungry. I wish we had some food," Marcus said. Instantly, there appeared a picnic hamper at their feet, together with a tablecloth set with food and drink: sandwiches, tea and cakes, strawberries and cream, and a separate bowl of as-sorted fruit.

They stopped, looking at each other, and then at the picnic. "Well, do we trust it to be safe? I feel as though I haven't eaten for days," Marcus continued.

June sat at the edge of the tablecloth and inspected the feast. "It seems real enough," she concluded. Marcus sat next to her.

A breeze rose and billowed through the wisps of a

nearby weeping willow, and when they lifted their heads, an old woman stood by the hamper. The lid raised itself slowly, and the food rose from the ground, hovered, and then filed into the basket, followed by the cloth, which folded itself neatly in midair before gliding into the hamper to cover the feast.

"As with most things, there is a price," the old woman wheezed. She was clad in black rags, and was stooped over a walking stick, gripped by gnarled fingers which had yellow, claw-like nails. Her face was shrouded by a tattered shawl.

"You are very hungry children, and, as you can see, I am able to satisfy your hunger," she continued.

"Old woman, what do you want from us in order that we may eat?" June asked.

"One of the three stones," she replied, "then you may eat forever."

Marcus checked his pockets and the stones nestled safely at his side. "Your price is too high. We will go without." He stood to confront the strange woman, but she turned away, and shuffled to the weeping willow where she stopped and turned, throwing back her head to release the shawl which then revealed the face of Ulah Ray. He cackled and pointed a mocking bony finger at them.

"Then let the nightmare continue!" The breeze returned as he vanished.

"He's left the hamper, Marcus." June lifted the lid.

"Be careful, June," he warned, as she lifted the cloth. At once, the air was filled with the sound of a swarm of furiously buzzing and beating wings, and from the hamper burst thousands of foul-smelling black flies which smothered them, sticking to their clothes, hands, and faces like filthy crawling tar.

Almost blinded by the frantic swarm, they staggered away from the hamper, beating at the flies while they ran, shaking their heads and slapping their clothes. Above the sound of blue-bottle buzzing, they heard Ulah Ray laugh once more.

The air cleared slowly as birdsong replaced the hum and panic. They approached a fountain where the water trickled, soothing and cool, into a pool where their fears seemed to wash away.

June stood at the water's edge, and looked down into the gently rippling lily-layered lake. "Marcus, look at this!" Her voice was urgent, and he ran to her side.

"Look down there." She pointed, and they both peered into a perfect mirror of nothing, for their faces were not reflected.

*"It's as if you don't exist here,"* a voice interrupted their astonishment.

"Oh no, I recognise that voice from another dream," Marcus groaned. "It's a He-Bride. We have to run, June. We must get away from here!"

He leapt from the edge of the fountain, but his

movement was a leaden slow-motion jump. "Come on, June!" Even his voice was burdened and slurred. The whole garden started to spin, gathering momentum like a carousel as fairground music, distorted by being played too slow, hit them giddily.

From the water, a row of lily-clad figures rose and shook themselves so that droplets cascaded like pearls. The He-Brides advanced like a small green army from the lake.

June looked back, turning her head agonisingly slowly. "Marcus, look!" she screamed.

"Fight the inertia—just concentrate on running!" he yelled. "This is dream pursuit paralysis: they will run at normal speed while we try to escape in slow motion. You have to will yourself to run faster; imagine using your arms to dig in like ski sticks to speed up—like this, watch."

He concentrated all his effort into forcing a large stride, spurred on by arms digging into the ground and pushing away so that one step was a glide of several metres. "It worked! I'm controlling my own dream."

"I can't keep up!" June struggled against the invisible net of slow motion—and all the time, the He-Brides advanced in a solid, steady march as the garden whirled giddily. Marcus willed her to move faster, to attack the paralysis and its magnetic barriers, and as June responded and began to draw away from her pursuers, her confidence grew and she increased speed, barely touching the lawn, so that he had difficulty keeping level with her.

"I think it's safe to stop now!" Marcus shouted above the noise of the hypnotic fairground organ.

As soon as they halted, the roar stopped, and the garden spun gradually to a standstill, spiralling dreamily in its return to normality. But when Marcus tried to walk at a regular pace, it felt as though the ground was rolling, just as if he was at sea. They stumbled together, unsteadily at first, pushing their way between figures neatly trimmed from hedges; baskets and birds, spheres and pyramids, until the green conspiring walls of the maze appeared once more to lead them deep and astray.

"George, Ed, John—where are you?" June called.

They strained their ears for a response, but none came.

"They must be in here somewhere," Marcus said.

"If they are, then they will be as hopelessly lost as us—hey, what's this?"

June kneeled to the ground, and picked up a sweet wrapper, on which was scribbled THIS WAY, with an arrow pointing in the same direction as they were heading.

"Marcus, this must have been left by them!" she exclaimed excitedly.

Marcus examined the wrapper suspiciously. "It

may have been," he agreed. "We're headed the same way, so let's see what happens."

They continued, and at the first intersection, another piece of paper lay against the blades of grass, marked simply with an arrow, and weighted down with a stone.

"Do we believe it or not?" Marcus wondered.

June replied with her feet and set off along the new path which twisted and turned, but did not branch off in any new direction, until it opened out onto a roundabout with three new paths from which to choose. This time, there was no clue.

"What can have happened to them?" Marcus searched anxiously for a sign, and again called out the names of his friends. As his words faded into the air, the ground shook with the trample of approaching hooves; an urgent canter drumbeat slapping the turf like the rhythm of life; a rumble growing closer, and bearing towards them with immense speed. In a shower of flying mud and grass, a great, white, one-horned horse sped along one of the paths like snow and silver in full flight.

"It's Prancer!" Marcus held out his hands to greet the Unicorn as it pulled up sharply, whinnying and pawing the air, its eyes full of swirling dreams. It circled them, stopped and stamped with its hind legs, then lowered itself to the ground.

"He wants us to get on," said June.

Prancer snorted as if in agreement, and shook his head so that his mane flared like a sparkling waterfall.

"I think you're right," Marcus agreed, and approached the Unicorn cautiously. Prancer snorted again. Marcus sat astride the great back, and June climbed on also, hugging the Unicorn's neck as he stood and selected a path, breaking quickly into a breathtaking canter so that the walls of the maze flashed by like blurred emeralds. And just as the roar and gust of the wind in their ears threatened to deafen, Prancer's feet lifted from the ground, and they became silent and airborne, his hooves dancing in flight, clipping the tops of the hedges, and carrying them away. As they looked back at the roundabout within the maze, the ground bubbled and boiled, sinking deep and blood red.

Prancer soared above the maze, taking them through sunset and midnight, dawn and midday, in a whirl and dazzle of colour. Slowly, he descended, and the horizon tilted. The whole earth seemed to turn itself inside out as they sank lower, brushing the tops of weeping willows which waved like seaweed trees caught in a deep ocean current; skimming the hedgerows, ducking and diving as they were returned to the Nightmare Maze. The great Unicorn touched down at a canter, nostrils flared, a powerful silver stride flashing across the grass and pink clover.

He pulled up in a flurry of turf, whinnied, and lowered his wise head, motioning for them to dismount.

June slid from his neck and hugged him. "Thank you, Prancer," she breathed, "but where are our friends?"

Thc Unicorn shook his head and pawed the grass while Marcus lowered himself to the ground. "Help us to find them and the way out," he pleaded.

Prancer side-stepped and neighed, his horn pointing to an intersection at their side.

"Is that the way, boy?" June asked.

Prancer snorted in reply, restless and eager to leave them now. He raised himself onto his hind legs.

"I think he wants us to go," said Marcus. "Come on, June." When they had reached the new path they turned to look back. Prancer had gone.

"Where is he?" June wondered.

They searched the sky, which turned momentarily from day to night, cold and star-clustered. They heard a ring of sleigh-bells and the crack of a whip, followed by a flurry of snowflakes and a split-second image of a Unicorn emerging as a reindeer to join a team pulling a sleigh.

When they blinked, it was daylight again, and the snow which had teased their faces quickly melted.

"We must be close to Christmas—we must be going home." Marcus felt a new energy, and a belief that the Challenge was drawing to a close. Yet, when they rounded the next corner, the shout of fresh conflict met them: a struggle on the lawn where George, Ed, and John were being stalked and circled by agitated stick-like figures. As they looked in horror, more figures unfolded and arose from a clump of bushes, springing into action with quick, aggressive movements; manic marching men closing in. And yet they did not notice June or Marcus.

"Ed, look out! Behind you!" June screamed, as one of the bush-men lunged from behind. Ed sidestepped just in time, narrowly avoiding contact with his tormentor.

George and John glanced sideways towards Marcus and June. "Help, they're closing in!" John ducked in mid-sentence as the branch of a limb raked his back, scrabbling for a hold. He twisted and pulled away, and the bush-man was left clutching a handful of ripped shirt.

They were now fully enclosed by the advancing figures who suddenly broke rank to form a box which trapped them against the wall of the maze. Then the line parallel to the wall stepped forward, ominous and menacing.

Ed tried to scramble his way over the hedge, but it bowed and quivered, a leafy conspirator in league with the bush-men who began to chatter excitedly. The advancing line halted, and one of the figures stepped forward a pace so that he was barely a metre from the three friends.

"Trade me the Balance for your freedom," he snarled.

"They don't have it. I am the Keeper!" Marcus stepped towards the leader of the bush-men, who turned slowly to face him.

"Then trade me the Balance for their freedom, Keeper!" He spat the last word as if he were ejecting venom from his mouth. To emphasise his intention, the line of figures stepped forward a couple of paces so that George, Ed, and John were obscured from view completely, smothered by the bush-men and the wall of the maze.

"I can't do that," he replied.

"Marcus, you must," June insisted. "There's no way out."

"Ten seconds, Keeper. Then my men will tear out the souls of your friends and trade them to Ulah Ray." The bush-man raised an arm, preparing the order to attack. "Five seconds, Keeper. Four, three, two..."

"Alright, alright, you win. Just let them go, please." Marcus reached for one of the stones.

"The Balance first, Keeper." The leader of the bush-men extended his other hand.

"Come on, Marcus; he only has a one in three chance of receiving the true stone," June whispered.

"Before I hand you the Balance, you will tell us the

way out."

"Very well." The leader pointed to the hedge opposite him, within which there were two openings like archways made from brambles.

"They're like the arches in the wood," said June. "It must be the way back."

Marcus agreed. "They look identical."

As he spoke, the bramble archways in the wood trembled and shook in a shower of snow, and in each there appeared a light like a guiding beacon—and when Marcus handed a stone to the leader of the bush-men, the light grew stronger.

The figures retreated while their leader examined his treasure, and George, Ed, and John ran forward.

"Quickly, through the arches!" June cried, and they sped towards the exit.

"Liar!" the leader of the bush-men thundered furiously. "This is a fake. Stop them, stop them!"

His warriors responded, but it was too late. The fugitives entered the left hand archway which bathed them in gold and bronze rays—and as the first wave of bush-men reached the exit, the archways lifted simultaneously as the entire group ran, crashing and uncontrolled, into the hedge, where they fell into a writhing heap.

# 19

# Owl House

Ed looked back as the entrance darkened and the sounds of pursuit faded. "We've lost them," he said, relieved. "How did you find us? We started to leave a trail, but we ran out of paper."

"If I told you we hitched a ride on a Unicorn, would you believe me?" Marcus laughed.

"It's as believable as being attacked by a clump of bushes," George replied. "How have you been? We've seen and felt everything in the Glimmersphere, but we didn't expect to be dragged into the last stage of the Challenge."

"It's been an ordeal, but hopefully the worst is over," Marcus replied. "How about you? How long have you been wandering in the maze?"

"We really don't know," said John. "It feels like a day or two, but the way time has been distorted during the Challenge, it might just as well be five minutes or a year."

"You've done really well—we're proud of you." Ed

slapped Marcus on the back as they walked, strong, together, and united.

"I've had plenty of help, although I could have used more." Marcus grinned.

It became dark, and the air grew noticeably colder as they walked, while the ground felt soft and powdery underfoot.

"It's snow!" John stooped to scoop a handful, and it was so fine that it crumbled between his fingers, and drifted back to the ground.

"We must be back in the wood." June quickened her pace.

"I'm freezing." John spoke between chattering teeth, arms wrapped around his chest in an attempt to ward off the stab of winter.

June and Ed burst through the end of the archway together, and stood blinking as they waited for their eyes to adjust to the gloom.

"Look, our coats!" Marcus pointed to the branch of a nearby tree where a row of winter clothing hung; and as they dressed, a full moon slid from behind the midnight grey clouds, illuminating the wood, and bathing the snow with a flood of pale light which enabled them to see and move between the trees.

At the edge of the wood, John gasped. "Look at this!"

In silence, they gathered, staring in awe at a building which had appeared next to the Lightning Tree in the middle of the field; a structure which resembled a church with a tall spire stretching skywards. When they craned their necks to follow its ascent towards the clouds, it seemed to grow higher and higher still, making them feel giddy. And, clearly visible above the entrance to the building, a sign blazed.

"Owl House. It's from my worst nightmare," Marcus groaned.

"It doesn't look too bad," Ed commented.

"No, but it contains my worst fear: the hidden, unknown horror at the top of the staircase, and it draws me higher and higher with manic, mesmerising music. I've never faced it. I've always woken up before reaching the attic at the top, but whatever lurks there is my ultimate terror."

*"One, two..."* A voice began a count which raced across the snow and filled their heads, loud and commanding.

"It must be Forty-Forty, the last stage of the Challenge," said George. "We'd better hide."

"From what?" asked June.

*"Seven, eight, nine..."* The count quickened.

"Let's move. I don't intend to stand here and wait for whatever is hunting us." John backed into the wood, knocking a snow-laden branch which quivered and sent a shiver of snow cascading around him.

"Remember, only I have to make it to base," Marcus whispered as they crept back between the trees.

"If we split up into two groups, one can act as a decoy while I make a break for the Owl House with the others."

"I didn't think you wanted to go inside. Why don't we face it together?" Ed asked.

"I don't have any choice," Marcus replied, "and anyway, it's my nightmare, so I'll just have to confront it."

"But not alone," June insisted.

"Twenty-five, twenty-six..." The count continued, gathering momentum like a snowball as they scrambled for cover, diving deeper into the heart of the wood.

At fifty, the count stopped, and faded to an iced whisper across the gallery of snow. At the rear of the wood, John, Ed, and June were crouched in a small hollow next to a holly tree, anxiously keeping watch, and waiting for sounds of pursuit; for the snap of a twig, the thud of a boot in the snow, or anything that might reveal a hunter's whereabouts. But all was still except for a few falling flakes.

Nearer to the centre of the wood, George and Marcus had selected a tree in which they were now perched about five metres above the ground; dark fugitive silhouettes pressed against the branches.

*"Behold, the slaves of the cavern!"* The voice of Ulah Ray thundered from the Owl House.

"What does he mean, Marcus?" George whispered.

"I don't know," Marcus replied, shifting uneasily on a branch which shook as he sought a more comfortable position.

"Keep still, listen!" George urged.

From the direction of the Owl House, there came a sound like that of a door creaking in a winter gale. Then a grating of metal and rust, followed by the beating of leathery wings riding the air. The shrill shriek of bats momentarily caught in the light of the moon as they circled the sky above the trees; bats the size of fully grown men turning across the night and swooping towards them.

"They're just like the guards in Ulah Ray's court room," said Marcus.

George nodded, his eyes fixed intently on the huge bats flapping above their heads. "Surely they can't track us; bats can't see well enough."

Suddenly, the circling formation broke, and the flapping of wings became louder as the bats dropped between the trees, systematically searching branches, twitching and shrieking, ever closer. George and Marcus hugged the trunk and tried to press themselves into the bark, to merge with the tree and become invisible, faces obscured by the hoods on their jackets.

One of the bats was nearly upon them, spiralling the trunk and beating snow from the branches, its claws even brushing Marcus's back, scratching and tearing as it passed, then dropping below them to hover just above the ground before selecting another tree.

"That was close," George whispered.

Marcus lifted his head slowly, feeling for the tear which raked across his back. "I hope the others will be alright," he said.

As the search continued towards the back of the wood, they lowered themselves cautiously. For a moment, the sound of approaching wings returned, and they froze once more—but the bat passed, and they continued their descent unhindered.

"Let's try to make a break from cover." George signalled, and they picked their way forward, leaving a trail of compressed footprints through the snow and between the silent, glistening trees.

In the hollow at the rear of the wood, the others watched in horror as the giant bats approached. Ed lay prostrate and tried to push and prise himself inside the prickly shelter of the holly tree—but it would not yield, and he retreated scratched and frozen from his endeavours.

John glanced over his shoulder to the adjacent field, and June read his thoughts.

"I know. It's the only place to run, and there's no cover," she said.

"They'll pick us off easily," he agreed; and resumed his attention towards the gathering leathery swarm.

The leading bat dropped without warning, plummeting downwards in a blur of wings and fur. Its claws carved through the snow, slashing powder like icing sugar into the air. In one swoop, it plucked and carried Ed away noiselessly into the night, and though he kicked and wriggled, it was a useless strugglc. And when the bat had cleared the trees, it circled once around the moon and released its prey. Ed screamed as he fell, snowbound and blinded by terror—but when he reached the ground, it was a soft landing, cushioned by his entry to the Glimmersphere where Carnyx and Thador hovered.

"You are safe, Ed," Thador comforted him. "You have performed well, have no fear."

In panic, John and June leapt from the hollow. John broke into a stumbling run across the open field where the thick mantle absorbed his efforts, consuming his energy and sapping his strength so that he was captured easily, plucked dizzy and breathless only fifteen paces from the perimeter of the frozen field to be trawled across the sky and dropped into the safety of the Glimmersphere.

June broke away to her left, keeping within the wood, yet hugging the periphery of trees and bushes. Only seconds before she would have reached the relative safety of the more dense middle section, a stray, tripping limb of root teased through the snow, and sent her sprawling. A slow-motion stumble from which she fought desperately to regain her balance, only to be snatched by claws clamped firmly on her shoulders as she was propelled upwards, kicking through the canopy of branches.

George and Marcus crouched in the cold, looking out across the field to the Owl House. The frontage was swelled by an enormous owl's head with eyes of searing saffron and coal. A huge hooked beak opened and closed while they watched, spilling vapour which unfurled like sickly fog over the snow.

"I think the beak must be the way in," George whispered.

"There's only one way to find out," Marcus replied.

Behind them, the sounds of pursuit grew louder as they once again heard the scratch and scuffle of re-turning claws and the beating of wings.

"They're coming back! Let's try to run to base." George scanned the moon-soaked windless field, and edged forward, cautiously at first, but soon gathering momentum. Marcus followed.

Far above the trees, a bat hovered, riding the winter sky like an enormous bird of prey ready to plummet and pounce upon its next victim, surveying the landscape in the flicker of the moon between the clouds. It detected movement the instant Marcus and George began to cross the field, their shadowy shapes leaving furrows in a snowy wake. And it swooped without making a sound, a lazy dive which knocked

George head-first and with arms outstretched as he skidded like a human torpedo.

"Keep running!" George yelled when Marcus turned to assist his friend. "Go on, you can make it!"

George scrambled to his feet as the giant bat circled him and dropped once more, its cries for help bringing a swift response from the returning reinforcements who shrieked in reply from the middle of the wood.

Marcus ran as fast as he could without tumbling, fighting the snow's cold caress as it absorbed the impact of his running.

"Keep going, Marcus, don't look back!" George's voice was above him as he was carried away—and now the sound of the returning bats, the hunters of the night, spurred him on even though the icy air rasped in his throat and burned his lungs. The Owl House was within reach, maybe just twenty paces away. It was at once both strangely alluring and nightmarish.

"Ascend your mind's throne." The beak spoke to him as it emitted more wisps of sulphurous vapour which crept into the night. Then it clamped shut.

As the wing-beats closed in, so near that he could feel them displacing the air, he zig-zagged like a yacht tacking; and two of the creatures screeched their annoyance as they sailed past, rising to circle and dive again. Another brushed his shoulder, and he shrugged it away, beating with his fists, swerving wildly and almost losing his footing. The bat whirled away in an ellipse to make a formation with the previous attackers.

The beak re-opened, beckoning. Another stream of sulphur singed the snow as Marcus reached it. Then it began to close, so that he was forced to dive and to lunge desperately with a bat screaming and scratching at his back as it struggled to lift him before colliding with the Owl House. It crashed heavily, clutching Marcus's coat, to lie twitching and bloody in the snow, until it twitched no more. And a trickle like a river of red rubies spread out over the ground.

# 20

# The Balance

Marcus lay sprawled upon a cold, hard floor of stone, shrouded by a blanket of mist which slowly lifted to reveal a tightly twisting spiral staircase. It seemed to climb forever upwards.

*"Ascend your mind's throne."* The voice of the Master of Thoughts spoke softly.

*"You will never ascend, you will never ascend!"* The voice of Ulah Ray breezed upwards in a sour wind through the rafters of a church roof.

*"Ascend your mind's throne."* The Master of Thoughts repeated.

Marcus began to climb—and as he did, a harpsichord waltz began to play in time to his footsteps; the manic, hysterical waltz of the living dead from his worst nightmare, summoning and hypnotising him upwards to the attic at the top of the stairs. He obeyed as in his dream; painful effort, sobbing, relentless, rising terror, torment, the pain of centuries in unseen eyes staring sullen and sad from wavering walls. Higher, still higher. In a torrent of fear, he climbed, silently obeying the lonely harpsichord. Until he reached the top, where the wooden floorboards, ancient and flaking, creaked—and a dull wind moaned across midnight moors, blowing through his tousled hair. He stood facing a door: the entrance to the attic where the ultimate unknown terror lurked.

The music stopped abruptly, and the whole floor breathed as if it was alive. The top of the stairs wavered precariously as Marcus stepped forward and knocked upon the door three times.

The door creaked and then swung open wide. "Three knocks, one for each of The Trinity." The Master of Thoughts smiled, and welcomed Marcus to the Chamber in the Great Diamond Dome on Future Earth—and as he entered, both sides glowed their respect.

As Marcus walked, his footsteps echoed in the cavernous great Chamber, and the Master of Thoughts faced him in the image of a man, cloaked in a white, flowing robe, and he spoke gently. "You have come far, Marcus, and you have arrived safely. The Challenge nears its conclusion, for it is time to replace the Balance if you can."

With arms outstretched, the Master of Thoughts shimmered backwards across the floor of the Chamber to a seat at the far side, where he sat as the Speaker of the House, exercising calm over both divisions, with an air of fairness and equilibrium. The diamond walls sparkled as Marcus continued to walk across the centre of the Chamber.

"But I have two stones!" he cried. "Which one is the real Balance?"

"You will make the right choice at the first attempt, have no fear. You will know, Marcus, you will know..." came the reply. He advanced further as a whirling pattern of kaleidoscopic gemstones flashed with the colours of the spectrum. The essence of centuries distilled seeped over him eerily as the parameters of history compressed and parted like an invisible sea of time. He recognised the pictures on either side from the images the Balance had revealed before Adam had made his final, fateful journey. Painted people in rows hung in time's gallery, evil staring at good; good staring at evil. And he came to rest at the Image; of sweet sorrow staring serenely from above, and beneath him, the inscription, A KISS IN TIME.

"Of course," Marcus gasped, "the kiss of betrayal."

Directly in front of the Image stood the empty thought pattern holder, and Marcus searched for the two remaining stones, placing them in the palm of his hand to turn over again and again, desperate for a clue by which to identify the true Balance.

Suddenly, he felt a splash, and one of the stones glistened in the diamond light. Marcus looked up at the Image as a tear rolled down its face, spinning like a pearl through space to splash on the same stone, and, without hesitating, Marcus leaned forward and replaced the Balance in its holder, restoring the power to the Light Side.

Instantly, the whole Chamber was flooded with light dancing brightly through the gilded walls. A great wave of goodness and tranquillity washed over him like summer sun and rainbows, golden and warming. And while he blinked in the dazzling display, his vision became blurred, the setting washed away like a reflection on water disturbed; rippling and breaking up; carrying him away gently, back through the wilderness hours, back through centuries of dust and dilemma, returning to Christmas and snow and home; and as he was catapulted through time's trembling walls, a voice pure and wise spoke.

*"Cherish life like the treasure of possibility."*

It was Christmas morning.

A sunrise wind swept up the winter birds like faded stars as Marcus stared from his bedroom window to the wood where the trees trembled. The two orbs hovered above the highest branches, as if undecided about their return journey.

He could sense Thador's thoughts, and then those of his friends as they stirred in their sleep, becoming numbly aware that good held the Balance, and that Thador and Carnyx were returning to Future Earth.

He could also sense the wise orb's thanks.

"Thador," he ventured, "did the Image ever come back?"

"No, I don't think so. Not yet, Marcus," the orb replied.

"How can you be so sure?" he asked.

"Because we are what you will become. We are the Next."

"Then the Master of Thoughts is the Father of the Image?"

"Yes, he is. Merry Christmas, Marcus, merry Christmas..."

Then there was a flash, and the orbs hissed and disappeared into the dawn.

*

The Chamber was in recess. It darkened gradually. There was a gentle hum of thought patterns which faded until all was silent, and the air sentry still.

The Chamber was deserted, save for one. No-one saw the obsidian figure approach the Image. Nobody saw the bony fingers as they swapped the stones. And no-one saw the shrouded figure as it left the Chamber, looking back once over its shoulder as another tear fell, only to boil and evaporate before it could splash to the floor.

"You are imprisoned while I roam free!"

Then Ulah Ray smiled, laughed uncontrollably, and slid into the shadows.

# About the author:

Martin Lott is originally from Horley in Surrey. Having spent time living in Perth, Western Australia, he is now a resident of Littlehampton in West Sussex. He is married with one son and two daughters. From Monday to Friday he works as a payroll officer for an NHS Trust. In addition to writing books he is a keen musician and songwriter. His play *The Condemned* was recently performed at the Courtyard Theatre in London.

# Also by Martin Lott:

## The Witchetty Men

*"The wind whispered something and chuckled. And in the middle of the nearest corn field there appeared a circle."*

The disturbance of sacred sites has triggered a signal. As the sequence of crop circles nears completion, Emily and Ben find themselves trapped in a conflict: the outcome of which decides the fate of Earth itself.

Time is running out...

Printed in Great Britain
by Amazon